I0760405

RECLAIMED

THE ADOPTED SERIES
BOOK THREE

MEGGAN LARSON

Library and Archives Canada Cataloguing in Publications.

For permissions contact:

hello@starfishstoriespublishing.com

E-Book ISBN: 978-1-990419-38-6

Print ISBN: 978-1-990419-39-3

Hardcover ISBN: 978-1-990419-40-9

Dust Jacket ISBN: 978-1-990419-69-0

1st Edition

Edited by C.B. Moore

Cover Designed by Meraki Cover Design

This series is dedicated to my (adoptive) dad, Scott. I wish we'd had more time together. I will always miss you. March 1949 - June 2024

To any transracial adoptee or mixed race person who has ever wondered who they were and where they fit in, this one is for you.

And to Harriet—thank you.

1

My roommate Ruby was dragging me by my coat behind a makeshift wall. My breath came in short, ragged gasps as though a noose had tightened itself around my throat. My fingers felt both numb and burning while displaying a shade of red I had never seen on them before. My eyes were mere slits as the brightness made a wider gap too painful. I felt around blindly for the sunglasses in my pocket as I continued to get pelted.

The wetness stung my face while my eyes leaked and I scrambled to get somewhere safe, but my feet didn't seem to be working properly. I stood to make a run for it, but before I could escape I was hit so hard in the face that I fell backwards. Staring up at the sky I willed myself to get up and fight back. *You can't let them win, not again.*

I flipped onto my hands and knees and crawled to safety. Then I prepared my weapon of choice: perfectly round, smooth, and deadly. Pressing it to my lips for luck, I stretched back my left arm and launched it through the air with all my might. I smiled as I heard the thud of impact.

"TAKE COVER."

I didn't know who'd said it, but I wasn't waiting to find out. I hugged my knees to my chest with my arms over my head like I was bracing for a plane crash or a grenade. Silence followed.

"Olivia? It's okay. It's over now."

I peered up at Ruby's extended hand and blinked back the flash of Lucas's face that swept across my mind as I let her pull me up.

"That was the roughest one yet," I murmured as I rubbed my sore cheek to assess the damage.

"You never get used to snowball fights at Carleton." Her voice held the wisdom of a seasoned warrior.

We exchanged grins and threw a wave at the other students. It was an unspoken rule that every fresh snowfall required a snowball fight. As soon as the first one was flung through the air, it was every man for himself. I loved it.

The sound of snow crunching under my boots filled my ears as we made our way across the quad and into the school. January in New York was very different from January in Florida, and this year had apparently been record-breaking for snowfalls.

"Do you have a class now?" Ruby linked her arm through mine as we crossed the cafeteria together.

I shook my head. "Not until this afternoon. I think I might go change and then head to Equator to grab a London Fog." Equator was the local coffee shop that most students preferred to frequent, and they made the best London Fogs, in my opinion.

Ruby's dimples deepened as she waggled her eyebrows at me. "You and your tea. I'll change too. I'm soaked and it feels like I wet my pants."

I snorted as we made our way to the dorm. Ruby's dark hair was braided, a chunk of hot pink at the very front and colorful cloth weaved throughout. She greeted almost every student we passed with a hearty laugh and a clap on the shoulder, which made our walk about ten times longer than it would have been on my own. After months of rooming with her, I was no longer surprised that she knew no strangers, and I didn't mind how long it took to get anywhere. The truth was, I had her extroverted nature to thank for many friends.

The common area in our dorm was always the longest part of any journey with Ruby, despite being the shortest distance to our room. We stepped over shiny, dark-stained hardwood floors in a hallway lined with abstract paintings until we reached the lounge area, where several students sat around playing cards and others made a snack in the small kitchen area. Here, we had a privileged view of the city skyline through several big windows. Ruby immediately began talking with the snackers, so I studied the message board and all the events and school clubs. An event for a writing club caught my interest, but I dismissed it when I saw they met during my sociology class. Ruby was already deep in conversation with a guy about the historic roots of slavery on Ivory Coast, so I unzipped my jacket—it was going to be a while before she was done.

I busied myself with the flyers while I waited.

Mathletes—a club for those brilliantly gifted in all forms of math. *Pass.*

The Artists' Way—a club for recovering artists. *I don't even know what that means.*

The Runners' Club—a club for...you guessed it, runners. *I like the sarcasm, but I'm already on the track team.*

Soul Care—peer support for victims of sexual assault. *Heavy. And yet...*

WITHOUT THINKING IT THROUGH, I grabbed a flyer for Soul Care and shoved it into my purse. A glance at my roommate indicated that she wasn't going to be finished anytime soon, so I snuck away to change into dry clothes and then headed down to the cafe on my own. I stepped off the elevator and into the dome. Everyone called it that because the ceiling was fifty-feet high and arched into a crystal-clear dome. There were benches for students along the wall and it was essentially the indoor hub for gossip and French fries. Ruby and I had enjoyed many late-night chats under the stars there—what you could see of them anyway; it was New York City, after all. Students were packed in like sardines and I made my way through the crowd dodging flying elbows and rogue backpacks.

"Liv, great job at the meet last week." Ben Packer was passing by and lightly touched my arm.

"Hey, you too, Ben." I bit my lip as soon as the words were out.

His lips turned down just enough to stab my heart with deserved guilt. "I came last in the 400-meter."

I reached up and ruffled his red hair affectionately. "True. But didn't you also have a personal best time in the 200-meter? That race is no joke."

His face brightened. "Yeah, I guess I did. Thanks, Liv."

My guilt subsided. "See you at practice tomorrow," I called after him as he waved and disappeared into the crowd.

I paused before the large doors that led out to the quad and moved off to the side so I wouldn't be in the way. I zipped up my coat, pulled my knitted hat down to cover my ears, and slid my hands into my mittens before going outside. The frigid air assaulted my throat on its way down into my lungs, and I let myself get used to the below-freezing temperature before heading down the stairs.

The snow was still falling, and I couldn't help myself. I stopped and tilted my head to the sky while holding my mouth open to catch flakes. They were cool on my tongue, and a giggle escaped me.

The walk to Equator was under five minutes, but I took my time. The path was hidden under a blanket of snow, and I watched a bluejay enjoying a snack at the bird feeder that hung from one of the rare maple trees in the city. Everything sounded muted, as though the snow created a hush everywhere it fell. New York was mostly a concrete jungle, yet patches of nature were strewn here and there. My face hurt from smiling.

The phone buzzed in my pocket, bringing me back to reality, but I kept walking without checking it; some moments were better left undisturbed by technology. Once I was seated at a table by the window with my tea—London Fog, three pumps of sugar-free vanilla syrup—I checked my messages.

There was a text from Mela and one from my sister Leah. I wrote Mela back first, and was still in awe at how strong she was after the death of her mom. She rolled her eyes every time I said it, but I could tell she appreciated the sentiment. Next, I wrote back to Leah. I commented on the latest family drama and encouraged her to say yes to the boy who had asked her to the dance. She was the best thing to come out of what I had gone through with Ali—other than G.G. A wave of grief passed through me momentarily, the way a fish breaks the surface of the water for just a second, causing a ripple, and then it's gone.

I missed her so much.

The sun was peeking through the clouds, making the fresh snow shimmer like shards of glass. I wasn't sure which view I preferred: The sun sparkling over the ocean had always been my favorite, but the way the light danced on top of the snow was otherworldly. It almost felt like being on some alien planet, and I loved the strangeness of it.

I sipped my drink and checked on the due date of a few assignments to make sure I still had enough time to complete them. A text from my birth father flashed on the screen, making me jolt in my seat.

Hey, baby girl, I'm going to be in NYC next week for work. Can you get together for a coffee? – Love, Jason

My hands cupped the hot mug as I pondered. Could I? Yes. Did I want to? I sighed. I did want to; I just never knew what to say to him. Wasn't it supposed to feel more natural with family? Easier? I set my phone on the table and continued to nurse my drink. I wasn't ready to answer him yet. I had had to wait eighteen years to hear from him. I figured he could wait a day or two to hear back from me.

2

"To what extent does our ethnicity affect our life chances? Get into pairs and discuss."*

Professor Hawthorne busied himself at his laptop while the theater-style sociology class erupted into dozens of private conversations.

"Remind me again why you convinced me to take this class?" I gave Ruby my best withering look.

She laughed. "Because sociology is so *fascinating*. It asks the meaty questions of life like 'why did slavery exist' so that we can learn from the past. Those that fail to learn from history are doomed to repeat it, after all."

Her arms were animated, and she pumped her eyebrows, making her gold eyeshadow shimmer in the light.

"Riiiiiight…" I wasn't convinced.

I shifted in the seat halfway up the auditorium, where we always sat. Professor Hawthorne was running his hand through his salt-and-pepper hair while tapping his pen against his coffee mug. He looked to be in his forties, and usually wore jeans and a T-shirt. Not exactly *professorly*, but I dug it.

"You needed another elective, and you get to spend an extra

hour and a half with me each week. That's reason enough, wouldn't you say?" Ruby's voice interrupted my thoughts.

Again I laughed, and knew she was right. My major was officially English, but I had to take a few electives, and Ruby was all too happy to rope me into a class with her. I looked at her sideways as she pulled out a pen and piece of paper, and was struck anew by how much looking at her was like looking in a mirror. Tanned skin? Check. Dark hair? Check. Athletic build? Check. The only obvious difference was the color of our eyes. Hers were golden honey and mine were green. She was wearing a bright green top with yellow and black accents; her wardrobe was much more colorful than my typical jeans with a black or white long-sleeve.

"You're doing that thing again," she said in a singsong voice.

"I know, I'm sorry. I'm just not used to being around people who look like me."

"What do you mean? Mixed?"

"Well, yeah. There were no *mixed* kids in my grade in Florida, and we lived in suburbia. My parents' friends were all White." My voice dropped at the word "mixed," as though it was a secret word I didn't want others to hear. Was it even okay to say that? I had no idea.

Her eyes were warm with a hint of sympathy. "So, you were the only Black kid in your classes?"

My face grew hot as if someone had suddenly shined a bright spotlight on me like in a police interrogation.

"No, I mean there was one actual Black guy." My voice shook slightly.

"Actual Black? What does that even mean?"

I blew out my breath before answering. "Well, I'm not *Black*."

"What are you, then?"

"I'm mixed."

"Me too. We're the same. Both Black. What am I missing here?" She leaned forward on her elbows and cocked her head to the side as she studied me.

"You could just as easily say I'm White. I'm half Black, half White." I mumbled the words under my breath.

She gaped at me. "So you identify as *White*?" She didn't sound critical as much as flabbergasted.

"I don't *identify* as anything. I'm just me. I'm mixed. Half and half." *But never whole.* I hadn't even realized I felt that way until the words popped into my mind. *I'm an imposter on either side, aren't I?*

"Didn't your adoptive parents introduce you to your culture?" Her face was so full of confusion it might have been funny, if I hadn't been so uncomfortable with the topic of conversation.

"Not really. I mean, I got a Black Barbie once."

"That's it? Damn, Liv. They, like, erased half of your history. Couldn't erase that booty, though." She leaned back in her chair and waggled her eyebrows mischievously.

"They didn't *erase* my history," I retorted, horrified. *They adopted me, took me in.* I didn't want anyone accusing my parents of anything untoward like that.

"They didn't introduce you to your culture either, did they? I thought I had it rough just being half Black, but at least I know where I came from and what kinds of things make me who I am."

Her eyes were full of pity, and I waited for the anger to bubble to the surface, yet it never came. The truth was, she'd just described exactly how I'd always felt but could never put into words. I looked away.

"Liv, I'm sorry. I didn't mean to upset you. I can be way too blunt for my own good." Her hand was on my shoulder, squeezing it gently.

"It's fine. Let's just talk about something else. Like, to what extent our ethnicity affects our life chances." I smirked to lighten the mood, but to my surprise Ruby's eyes darkened.

"Half of my ethnicity is Ivorian. Ivorians had no chance to be anything but slaves until a few generations ago."

"Geez, Ruby, I'm sorry."

She threw me a glance. "Sorry? The Black side of your family was probably in the same slave boat."

My stomach dropped like cables snapping in an elevator. I dismissed it almost before the words were out of her mouth. *No, that's crazy. Someone would have told me...right?* But who would have? My parents knew nothing about Jason's history, and Ali certainly wasn't going to offer up any information—if she even had any.

The class went on, with Professor Hawthorne instigating a few more topics of conversation. After twenty minutes of Ruby and I debating whether the constant change in society was an illusion—I decided it was all an illusion—I remembered that Jason was coming to town.

"Are you gonna see him?"

I frowned. "Yeah, probably."

"You don't seem very excited about it." Her tone was gentle.

"It's not that I don't want to see him. It's just really awkward when I do. I never know what to say, and we're just so different." I felt I had to explain myself so she didn't think he was some kind of jerk. He was actually nice; we just didn't seem to connect all that well, and I couldn't help but feel that the awkwardness was all my fault.

She nodded her understanding. "Maybe it'll be different this time."

I tried to take comfort and encouragement from her words.

"Okay, class, great job with the discussions."

The room grew quiet as Professor Hawthorne began to speak. Though his nature was pretty laid back, he had a way of commanding the room without ever having to raise his voice.

"This semester you will each do a presentation in front of the class worth fifty percent of your grade."

It got so quiet I heard someone's stomach rumble.

He went on to read from a sheet he was holding. "You can choose from the following five topics: the sociology of reproduction and change, the sociology of power relations and inequalities, the sociology of racism and slavery, the sociology of culture, or the sociology of processes by which social structures are maintained and transformed. I've made these vague on purpose so that you can really dig in and expand on your topic of choice. Presentations will begin in April. Come see me during office hours if you need help."

The sound of theater chairs flipping back up echoed around the room as students collected their things and stood to leave. I sat frozen in my seat. How was I going to do an entire presentation on topics I didn't even understand?

LATER THAT NIGHT, I sat on my bed staring out the window. Ruby's bed was untouched because she was at the party I had opted out of. I messaged Jason back and we made plans to meet for coffee the following week. Watching the snowflakes fall in the glow of the streetlights made me shiver at the thought of being outside. It was at times like this that I missed Florida and the soothing sounds of the ocean.

I pressed the starfish necklace to my lips and let it fall back on my chest. I missed him. I missed Mela and Nate too. I flipped through pictures of the four of us on my phone and didn't restrain the few tears that fell. I'd known it wouldn't be easy to come here and reinvent myself, but I hadn't expected to miss them all so much.

Taking the sheet from my sociology class with all the topics, I stared at it, willing myself to choose one until my eyes grew so heavy that I lay down instead.

I think I'm in over my head.

3

"I'm sure he'll be here any minute." I wasn't sure, actually, but I also wasn't about to admit that to the waiter who was on his third round of refilling my water.

He looked at me like I was being stood up on a date, and the sting of embarrassment burned in my stomach. I glanced around the restaurant Jason had chosen. I had never been there before, but somehow it felt familiar. It was a bright sunny day, and the restaurant had a family-owned-for-several-generations vibe to it, with lights hanging over every booth and a large jukebox playing a catchy song from the seventies. Bowls of peanuts were on every table, and I had created a pile of shells and uneaten peanuts in front of me. I was seated at a booth facing the door and saw him the moment he walked in.

A mix of relief and annoyance swept through me as I watched him greet the staff like they were old friends. He was in beige khakis and a white-collar shirt, and his gaze swept the room, looking for me. Once our eyes met, his face lit up; he grinned and sauntered over to me. I smiled politely, and to my surprise he came right over to my side of the booth and pulled me up into a hug. I stiffened at the sudden closeness of a man I hardly knew but tried to force myself to relax in his embrace. It was only for a few seconds, but I held my breath as long as it lasted.

Eventually he pulled away but kept his hands firmly around my arms, looking me over until he seemed satisfied. He nodded slightly and turned to sit on his side of the booth as I gratefully sank into mine. After we had placed our orders, the silence between us grew to a level so uncomfortable that I blurted out the first thing that popped into my mind.

"How's Kimmie?" My face flushed with instant regret as I remembered the jealousy that had nearly consumed me while watching him and his niece together.

If he noticed the shift in my body language, he didn't let it show. "She's great. She'll be starting her senior year in the fall, so she's really beginning to focus on her schoolwork and make sure she's in the best shape for college." He beamed with pride, the way any doting father would. Only, he wasn't her father; he was supposed to be mine.

I wondered if I'd ever get over the jealousy. Did I even have the right to feel that way? I wasn't sure. I took a sip of water to relieve the desert my mouth had become, but it did little to alleviate the discomfort.

"So, how's school?" Jason seemed unaffected by my awkwardness, and I threw him a grateful glance.

I caught him up on my classes, roommate, and how much I loved the snow and hated the cold in equal measure. He laughed easily.

"And Lucas? How's he doing?"

His words sent an ache into my chest.

"We broke up." It sounded hoarse in my ears. I hadn't talked about him in months, though Mela had continued trying to bring him up.

"Oh." He didn't mask his surprise. "I'm sorry to hear that. You two seemed really solid together." He took a long sip of his black coffee as I shoved my thoughts back into the Lucas-shaped hole in my heart.

"You must have questions for me. You've hardly asked me anything since we met." He leaned back in his seat and rested his right arm on top of the booth.

My mind went blank. The only question that came to mind sounded so ridiculous that I didn't dare say it out loud: *I don't know what it means to be Black.* I didn't think he'd understand. He was gazing at me expectantly, and my feet tapped a nervous rhythm against each other. *There's no place like home* ran through my head, nearly causing me to laugh.

"Where do I come from?" I finally said.

"How do you mean?" His eyebrows creased together as he took another long swig of his cooling coffee.

"Well…" I fumbled over my words but continued. "Where are our ancestors from? I've always been asked what I am, but I've never had an answer, ya know?"

He nodded with understanding. "Ah, yes. I've been asked a time or two myself."

His eyes sparkled with humor but not as though he was laughing at me. It was more like we were sharing an inside joke. I smiled shyly in response.

"My father's side of the family came from Africa. Nigeria, Sierra Leone, and the Ivory Coast, I believe, then through to Canada and eventually back into the US. My great-grandmother was Indigenous but lost her status when she left her community to marry a German settler." He stroked his chin thoughtfully.

"She left her tribe for love?" It came out as a whisper.

"Well, I mean, there was a lot of suffering in indigenous communities at that time. She could have simply wanted a better life for herself. It may not be as romantic as all that."

I wrinkled my nose. That sounded so…selfish. She left her entire community not for love, necessarily, but because she wanted better? Losing your indigenous identity over that just didn't seem worth it to me. I had a sudden thought. "Wait, *Canada*? How did your father's ancestors end up in Canada?"

Jason's eyes brightened. "Now *that* is very interesting. You've heard of Harriet Tubman?"

Her name was familiar, and I knew it had something to do with slavery and…some kind of railroad? I shook my head in defeat.

"I'm actually really proud of our ancestors. The way they risked their lives, and to go down in history connected with someone as extraordinary as Harriet Tubman…I've been collecting information about my family's history for years. I'll send you some of it, if you want. It's been somewhat of a passion project of mine for a long time. When you grow up like I did, familial history becomes very important." He was looking at me and I didn't want to rain on his parade, so I agreed with more enthusiasm than was honest.

"Sure, that sounds great." His eyes were still searching my face, and the feeling of being under a microscope was unnerving. I took a sip of the milkshake that had been sitting untouched in front of me. The sweet taste of strawberry was comforting, and I relaxed a little in my seat.

We spoke of school and New York for a while, and he took care of the check when the time came. As we stepped outside into the biting cold, the traffic was heavy and the sidewalks littered with brown slush. The sound of tires sloshing through puddles filled the air. It looked like it was going to snow again; the sky was gray.

"Thanks for doing this, baby girl." Jason pulled me into another hug and, again, I stiffened at the embrace.

Annoyance coursed through me as I pulled away. "Can I ask you something?" My tone came out a little harsher than I'd meant, and he drew back.

"Sure." His own tone was uneasy, and he appeared to brace himself for my question.

"Why didn't you look for me?" I was shocked at the words that flew out of my mouth.

"You waited until we were leaving to ask me that?" He

seemed hurt. The question hung in the air between us like the pressure that mounts before a storm. He avoided my gaze as he answered. "I—" He stopped, then started again: "I wasn't in a place to be there for you." He seemed to be struggling. "Losing you—" He choked on his words, cleared his throat, and continued, "Losing you was the hardest thing I've ever gone through, and it nearly destroyed me."

He shuffled his feet awkwardly like he was winding himself up to run away. All I could do was stand there motionless, as if I were before a wounded animal that spooked easily. One wrong move and he'd be gone.

"I was a mess, Olivia. Do you think I *wanted* to give you away?"

The change in his tone caught me off guard. My foot took an involuntary step back, away from his accusation.

"No, I don't think that," I replied carefully.

He moved toward me, his eyes seeming to plead with me to understand. "I had to pick up the pieces of my life slowly and get sober. I'd have been no good to you as broken as I was."

I nodded as though I understood what he was saying, but the little girl inside of me had always just wanted her daddy to look for her. It wouldn't have mattered to me what shape he was in when he found me.

He folded one hand over the other and dug his nails into the back of his wrist, the way I did when I was stressed. It wasn't noticeable, really; most people wouldn't have seen it, but I recognized the movement and felt guilty for bringing up the conversation.

"Look," he started, looking up at the sky; he made himself look at me again while continuing. "Rock bottom isn't a place I would wish on my worst enemy. But—" He cleared his throat a few times and blinked so hard I thought he might be having a stroke. Finally, he got the words out. "I never forgot about you." His shoulders sagged and he looked away, as if needing a minute to collect himself.

A lump formed in my throat, preventing me from responding. I watched him transform from a tall and confident man into a weary one, broken by the weight of his past. I wished that I could take my question back—reverse the last few minutes of our lives and never ask him why he didn't look for me. I could see now how selfish it was to ask, though necessary to me. I had never bothered considering what he had gone through by losing his only child. My thoughts had only been about myself and my pain.

"I'm sorry," I whispered finally. Sorry I had asked and sorry for the anguish he'd gone through because of Ali's actions.

"Me too." He squeezed my shoulder, hailed a cab, and jumped into it like it was his getaway car.

I stood on the sidewalk staring down the street long after his cab had disappeared.

4

"Now, Jackson!" Coach Grant yelled into the megaphone and clapped her hands together once, signaling the time had come for me to step it up and finish strong.

I rounded the three-hundred-meter mark of the indoor track and flew into the straightaway well ahead of my teammates. Determined to forget about my talk with Jason, I forced all my focus into pumping my arms and legs in perfect unison as the balls of my feet pounded down the last bit of the track. I crossed the finish line a solid twenty meters ahead of even my closest competitor, and the smile on Coach Grant's face was contagious.

She waved me over to where she stood on the side of the track. "Fantastic job, Olivia. You keep getting faster and faster. Keep this up and you'll be anchoring the 4x100-meter relay next track meet."

She clapped me on the shoulder, and I couldn't wipe the grin off my face as I jogged around the track for the cool down.

Anchoring the relay was a huge honor, in my opinion. The anchor was the last chance the relay team had to win the race and, as far as I knew, freshmen rarely got the chance to do it. I ran another lap to burn off the extra adrenaline coursing through my body and let my eyes wander around the track that had become my second home since it had gotten too cold to practice outside. The lanes were black and red like everything else in the school. Though it was a full 400-meter track, there were only six lanes instead of the normal eight, and in the center stood a large soccer field. A huge white dome enclosed the entire thing. I preferred the outdoor track with the bleachers and smell of freshly cut grass, but I figured it would be pretty hard to run through a foot of snow without breaking a leg, so the indoor track would have to do.

I took a quick shower and changed in the dressing room. A few of my teammates clapped me on the back with a "Good job" here, and a "Get it, Jackson" there. I really liked my new team and was grateful that Coach Grant was more like Coach Stewart than Coach Addison. I found I was much more motivated by encouragement than tear-downs.

Just as I was hitching my duffel bag onto my shoulders to leave, my phone rang with a private number on the display. I watched it ring, intending to let it go to voicemail, but changed my mind and answered it at the last second.

"Hello?" My voice was wary, expecting some kind of horn telling me I had won a cruise.

"Miss Jackson?" A man's voice came on the line and sounded official.

"Yes?" I sat down on the bench slowly.

"It's Officer Schmidt. Do you…remember me?"

Memories flooded my mind. Sitting in his office at the police station, telling him about my ex-boyfriend's attempted assault in an effort to get Lucas out of jail. Having him tell me I might be able to convince Chris not to press charges and warn me to be careful about going to confront him at the hospital. The sound of Chris' skull slamming against the pavement.

"Of course," I answered soberly.

"I'll get right to the point then. I'm calling to ask if you would be willing to testify against Chris Jamieson in court."

The air dropped out of my lungs like someone was using them to play the bagpipe. "Wh-what?"

I heard him sigh softly. "I know, and I'm sorry to be calling you about this. He is being charged by the state with at least one count of aggravated sexual battery and is facing no less than nine years in prison if convicted. The prosecution has a few witnesses willing to testify, and I believe your testimony would really help ensure he gets the justice he deserves, considering you were under eighteen when he attacked you."

Was the air getting thin? I was struggling to breathe. "I'm not in Florida anymore. I go to school in New York City," I stammered.

"Would you be willing to fly back to testify? This is important. Though I know it's not an easy decision to be faced with." He trailed off, letting me gather my thoughts.

It wasn't a hard decision at all, and yet it was an impossible choice. *Everyone will know what happened. You'll be seen as a victim, Liv; do you really want that? Are you really ready to be in the same room as Chris again?* The thoughts were pelting me like a hailstorm. "Can I—" My words caught in my throat. "Can I have some time to think about it?"

"Of course. The trial is in a couple of months. If you decide to testify, you'll need to come back before then to prepare with the prosecution team." He hesitated but then went on, "Olivia, if you do this, it isn't going to be easy. Chris's lawyers are going to do everything they can to discredit the victims. You would need to be ready for that."

My stomach twisted. I had seen enough court cases in movies to imagine myself on the stand, having my life picked apart in front of everyone I knew. It sounded like torture.

"I'll let you know what I decide." The crack in my voice betrayed me.

He left me the number where I could reach him, and the line went dead. I looked up and stared at my reflection in the mirror. My face was pale, and my lips tight. My eyes had become a sickly, mossy green, as if I were staring into a stagnant pond on an overcast day. The muscles in my arms flexed involuntarily, remembering the way *he* had held me down. How bad would it get if I went back?

Beads of sweat that had nothing to do with track practice pooled on my forehead. A moment of panic swept through me as I realized I would have to tell my parents what had really happened with Chris if I decided to testify. I had hoped to keep that buried forever, which would become impossible unless I said no. Imagining them watching my buried secret get pulled out of me on trial made me want to throw up.

How was I to make this kind of decision?

Back in my dorm room, I sat cross-legged on my bed watching the minutes pass on my phone. I had dialed my parents' number more than once but couldn't bring myself to press send.

I hadn't made any kind of decision, but the call with Officer Schmidt had rattled me, and I wanted to hear their voices. Things between us—especially with my mom—were still awkward. I hadn't even gone home for Christmas, though that decision had had more to do with feeling completely unprepared to face anyone I had left behind. *Stop being a coward, Liv.*

I pressed send.

"Liv, hey! How's it going, ya little rat?" The laughter in my dad's voice was contagious.

"Hey, Dad, I'm good." I laughed.

We chatted easily for a few minutes as I answered his questions about my classes. It was going so well that I decided to test the waters.

"I might come home for a couple of weeks in the spring, if that's cool," I said.

The pause on his end was so long that I pulled the phone away from my ear to make sure we were still connected.

"Why?" was his eventual question.

"I'll tell you if I come home, Dad." I regretted bringing it up. Clearly, our relationship was still in a precarious place.

A heavy sigh assaulted my ears from the other end of the line. "*More* secrets, Liv?" He didn't bother masking his disappointment.

"I'm not trying to keep—"

My mother's voice in the background interrupted me: "This is *just* like with Jason."

Shame flooded me and my shoulders drooped. "I've gotta go, Dad. Tell Mom I said hi." I ended the call before they could respond and turned off my phone.

They were never going to get over the fact that I'd looked for —and found—my biological father behind their backs after they'd told me to stop. Tears burned my eyes with the unfairness of it. They didn't—couldn't—know what it felt like to believe that you might be sent back like a puppy. That you might be dropped at the first sign of trouble or any kind of flaw. Only an adoptee knew what it felt like to be adrift this way. It was not fair that they were still punishing me for finding Jason, and I wondered how long they were planning to hold it against me.

The door opened and Ruby shuffled in with an armful of books nearly teetering out of her grip. My eyebrows rose, and she merely shrugged and plopped them on her bed.

"Why are you sitting in the dark?" She turned on her lamp without waiting for a response.

I hadn't even noticed. "What's all that?"

"For the sociology project. And"—she gave me a sheepish grin—"a little light reading."

I snorted. There must have been a dozen books on her bed, ranging from a couple hundred pages to thousands. I wasn't sure how she had even carried them all there herself.

"Donte helped most of the way." She waved her hand airily, as though reading my mind. Her on-again-off-again boyfriend must be on for now.

"What did you choose for your topic?" I mumbled. I hadn't even thought about what I was going to pick yet.

"The usual. The history of slavery, some of what my ancestors endured being from the Ivory Coast, plus a little White saviorism to round it off."

"The usual?"

"I've been researching this stuff since I was a kid. Being half Ivorian means more to me than speaking French and having my mother sew *gris gris* into my clothing against my will." Her words didn't match the loving tone of her voice.

"Gris gris?" I had never heard the term before.

"Yeah, it's like...what would you call it in English? An amulet, I think." She opened her gold jacket to reveal a material cross that had been discreetly sewn into the side.

"I didn't peg you for the religious type."

"Oh, I'm not. But it never hurts to cover your bases." She winked and turned her focus to the pile of books gathered on her bed.

I laughed and pulled out my blow dryer.

"Hey, Liv?" Ruby was eyeing me thoughtfully.

"Mmhmm?"

"Why don't you ever leave your hair curly?"

My hand froze with the blow dryer halfway to my head. "Honestly? I don't really know how to style my curls. Straight is the only way I know how to avoid a permanent bad-hair day."

Her eyes grew wide. "*That's* why? I guess that makes sense, actually. Who would have ever shown you how?" She tapped her chin, deep in thought.

"Right." I shrugged even as a wave of sadness washed over me. Just one more part of my culture I'd never learned.

Ruby snapped her book closed. "Okay, then, let's get to it." She hopped out of bed and pulled me into the bathroom. "First things first, it looks like your hair is between a 2C and a 3A, does that sound right?" Her head tilted as we looked at each other in the mirror.

"Huh?" I had absolutely no idea what she was talking about.

"Okayyyyy. What brand of leave-in conditioner do you use?"

"None." I bit my lip, guessing I was supposed to use some.

"This is worse than I thought… But it's okay!" she added quickly as she caught the look on my face.

The next forty-five minutes were spent deep-diving into all things hair. It was the tutorial I never knew I needed but somehow always wanted. Ruby showed me exactly how to care for my curls, and even gave me a bunch of styling products to use and keep. By the end of the night, I had the kind of hair I had always envied on other girls who looked like me. Catching Ruby's eye in the mirror as she marveled over my hair, I smiled shyly.

"Well, damn, maybe I shouldn't have helped you out like this. I might have just created my biggest competition." Her fake grimace made me laugh out loud.

"That's right, Ruby," I teased. "You'd better grab your man because I'm on the prowl." I tossed my hair suggestively.

She shoved me hard, and I nearly fell off the chair.

"Don't think I'll go down without a fight." She gave me her most menacing glare while shaking her fist at me, and we burst into laughter, still looking at each other's reflection in the mirror.

I might not have had the best relationship with my parents for the time being, but at least I had a roommate who made it impossible for my pity parties to last for too long.

5

I spent the next few days going through the motions but feeling more like a zombie than anything else. The implications of Officer Schmidt's words weighed heavily on me. *Chris's lawyers will do everything they can to discredit the victims.*

Sitting on a bench in the dome, I put my right hand over my left and dug my fingernails into the back of my wrist, welcoming the sting of pain to snap me out of spiraling. I hated that guys like Chris were out there, destroying women's lives.

The sound of students walking and laughing, the thud of doors opening and closing, even the smells wafting from the cafeteria were all lost on me as I struggled over whether I should return to Florida. I glanced at the time and quickly gathered my things, heading to a more secluded part of the university I had only been to once to speak to a professor during office hours.

The door in front of me was cream colored and slightly ajar with a poster on it that read:

SUPPORT GROUP FOR SURVIVORS

In-person peer support group for survivors of sexual violence.

I had been thinking about it ever since I had seen the flyer in our common room. Now more than ever, it felt like I should be around other women who had faced what I had with Chris. Hear their stories and maybe share a bit of my own.

Knocking softly, I poked my head in to find an older woman with graying hair and kind eyes behind square-rimmed glasses shuffling some papers. She smiled warmly and beckoned me into the room. A dozen chairs behind her formed a circle with a few girls already sitting spaces apart from each other. Each looked uncomfortable as they fidgeted in their seats.

"Should I?" I whispered as I pointed to the circle.

"Yes, yes, please go ahead and take a seat. We'll be starting in just a minute." She spoke softly and looked at her watch.

I took a seat next to a girl in ripped jeans and a long-sleeve shirt. She was leaning forward just enough for her long black hair to cover her face while her leg bounced up and down. I tried to throw her an encouraging smile, but she couldn't see it. Yet, somehow, I knew this was where I needed to be.

Two more seats were taken and then the door was closed, and the meeting started.

"Hi, everyone, I'm Professor Powell, but you can call me Kelly. I'm here more as a facilitator than anything. You've all experienced something that no one should ever have to, and I want to commend you on your courage for showing up at all. Would anyone like to share a bit of their story?"

An awkward silence fell over the room, and I was sure that if a pin dropped across campus, it would have sounded like a gunshot. Everyone looked anywhere else but at each other, and I surprised myself by clearing my throat.

"Umm, I can go first, I guess." I felt driven by the need to ease their discomfort, even if just for a moment. "My name is Olivia, and a while ago my boyfriend at the time tried to force himself on me. I managed to escape, but not without scars." I looked down while the pit in my stomach grew as steadily as the silence in the room. What if she had simply been asking for us to share something fun about ourselves? *You just had to go first, didn't you?* I chided myself.

"Thank you, Olivia. I believe you." Kelly's voice sounded grateful and determined. I risked a glance at her and smiled cautiously as our eyes met. I wondered why she said she believed me. No one had ever questioned my story, so it felt like an unnecessary addition.

"I was eleven the first time it happened." A hushed silence enveloped the room as the girl with the black hair began speaking. "My mom's boyfriend was babysitting me, and my little sister, and he caught me sneaking a cookie after bed. Let's just say I got more than a spanking."

Her hair continued to cover her face, but I didn't miss the tear that fell on her jeans, even as she quickly covered it with her hand. I had to stop myself from reaching towards her.

"Thank you for sharing. I believe you." Kelly's voice was hardly above a whisper.

For the next forty-five minutes, I listened as each girl told her story—some so awful it made what I went through with Chris seem like a dream in comparison. After each, Kelly thanked them and told them she believed them. The more she said it, the more I understood why. Judging by the reaction from some of the girls, it was the first time they had heard those words after sharing their experience. My feet felt as if they had been encased in lead as I imagined not being believed when I told Mela and Lucas. It was awful enough to have gone through what I had, but not being believed? I couldn't fathom it.

The more I heard, the more uncomfortable I became. These women had all been assaulted, probably by men who weren't reported, just like I hadn't reported Chris. If I had never pressed charges, did I really have the right to go back and testify? Wouldn't they just assume that it couldn't have been that bad if I hadn't done anything about it?

Professor Powell was wrapping things up. "When we share our burdens with each other, we give each other permission to heal. When we bring our hidden experiences into the light, the darkness has less of a hold on us. I'm proud of each of you. I'll see you next week."

Everyone shuffled out, some faster than others, until I was alone with Professor Powell.

"Something on your mind, Olivia?" She still smiled and folded her arms as she took me in.

"I want to help."

"Okay... How so?"

"I want to work with the other victims. Help them." The words had come out before I had even processed them, but I knew they were true. The women in that room were still crushed by their nightmares. I had learned to heal, and I needed to find a way to help. And I understood that a part of me was probably trying to appease the guilt I felt, but I figured it was for a good cause.

"But you're just as much a victim of sexual violence as they are." She looked confused.

"Not anymore," I replied, my voice low—steely, even. *I am not a victim—not anymore.*

She didn't seem to be convinced.

"Please. I want to learn how to do this. I think I'm leaning towards a career where I can help people like this in a tangible way." That bit of information was news to me, but my eyes implored her to let me help.

"How did you deal with it when it happened?" She asked in a way that made me think I was being tested.

I decided that honesty was the best policy. "With a lot of support from my friends." I smiled to myself, remembering how Mela and Nate had been there for me. "And when my ex started stalking me, my boyfriend protected me and helped me feel safe again. After my ex tried to blackmail me to get back together with him, I stood up for myself and he left me alone."

Her eyes widened, but she looked satisfied with my answer. She sat on her desk. "Well, I won't be able to let you counsel them; not yet, anyway. But I can take you on as a sort of intern if you want."

"Yes, I want that." I had cut her off without meaning to.

She smiled. "You may want to let me finish before you volunteer as tribute. I meant having you do things like printing flyers, making calls, organizing events, finding guest speakers, stuff like that. The truth is, I could really use the help. Still interested?" Her eyebrows were raised like she was expecting me to back out.

"I am. Definitely."

She nodded and took down my contact information with a promise—or threat, I wasn't quite sure which—that she'd be in touch soon.

LATER THAT NIGHT, as I walked through the snow back to campus with a latte from Equator in hand, I felt more alive than I had in months. I couldn't stop thinking about the stories the girls had shared. My heart ached for them, which only strengthened my resolve to help. I couldn't erase the scars Chris had given me, but I was damn well sure not going to let them go to waste.

6

A couple of weeks went by, and I was still no closer to choosing a topic for my sociology project. I was doing well in the rest of my classes, so the lack of progress with sociology had begun to stress me out.

With my laptop open in front of me, I sat in the common room, having decided to be more social. Ruby had spent almost every night in the library lately—since our room wasn't big enough to hold all the physical books she seemed to need instead of Google—but for once she kept me company. A few students played cards, and two guys laughed hysterically while playing Wii tennis. I was starting to think it might not have been the best place to choose a category for my project.

Out of the corner of my eye, I saw an email come through from Jason and clicked on it.

Hey Olivia,

Sorry it took me a while to get this to you. Here is some more information about your ancestors and how they wound up in Canada. Let me know if you have any questions or anything.

Jason

. . .

I DIDN'T MISS that he called me Olivia instead of baby girl, but I chose to let it slide, hoping that eventually we'd get past the awkwardness of our last in-person conversation. I had already looked up Harriet Tubman, a former slave who had personally led between sixty and seventy slaves to freedom through the Underground Railroad in the 1800s.

Opening the attachments, I could see that he had sent me old medical records written by hand. There were also newspaper articles, birth and marriage certificates, a census from 1851 and 1861, digitized photographs, and more.

"Whoa, check this out." I turned my laptop to Ruby and she leaned in.

"Dang," she said after scanning a few documents with her eyes. "Let me know if you find anything good."

She went back to her books, and I started clicking on the attachments.

The first one was a copy of the handwritten medical records for a woman called Mary with dates ranging from 1851 to 1862. I noticed that her initial last name, Booker, was changed to Pritchard in 1853, and I realized with a start that these were the medical records of my great-great-great—I wasn't sure how many greats it was—grandmother. She had run away through the Underground Railroad as a teen, and as I scoured through her medical records, my skin began crawling as if I had been thrown into a pit of snakes.

A broken arm that hadn't healed properly and scars all over her back from being whipped repeatedly were just two of the horrors she had endured. She had been branded on the shoulder like cattle and had deep scars on one of her ankles from being shackled. She had also nearly died from sepsis during her first pregnancy at seventeen. *She must have run away while pregnant,* I thought.

A note on the medical record indicated that her last name of

Booker wasn't her real last name; it had been assigned to her ancestors by their slave owners and passed down. *They didn't even have their own names.* I had always felt erased but this…this was so much worse.

I made myself continue. Mary had gone on to become an assistant nurse to a doctor who helped freedom seekers. Personally, I liked that term better than *escaped slaves.* I clicked on an old, digitized photograph of Mary with the doctor and his team of freedom seekers—and Harriet Tubman, who had personally escorted them to Canada.

"Holy crap!" I startled Ruby, who—now I saw—was the only other person in the common room.

"What? What?" She was looking all around as if expecting someone to jump out at her.

"Harriet Tubman helped my ancestor escape to Canada. Like brought her there herself."

"How do you feel about that?" Ruby asked thoughtfully.

"I mean, it's pretty crazy, isn't it? She brought her family and friends. That means my ancestor was *friends* with THE Harriet Tubman. That's crazy." I knew I was repeating myself, but I couldn't help it.

"It really is, Liv. That's quite a legacy you've got there." She smiled and went back to what she was doing.

The next picture of Mary and her family was from 1861. Someone had written the children's names and ages below the photograph. *Jason (10), Robert (8), Maria (4), John (7).*

Mary stood beside her husband, who was listed as William Pritchard. And all these years later, Pritchard was still Jason's last name. Mary was beautiful, and yet something in her eyes was haunting. And were they the same shape as Jason's? The set of her mouth seemed familiar, like I had seen him make that face. No, of course I was dreaming. The picture had been taken several lifetimes ago.

Her smooth dark skin matched that of her husband's, and as I peered more closely at her children in the picture, I became puzzled. Her oldest son, William, had considerably lighter skin than she did. A bead of sweat dripped down my back and the fingernails on my right hand were digging into the back of my left wrist again. I noticed it but wasn't sure why I was feeling so uneasy. Looking at his age again, I could sense that my brain was taking way too long to put two and two together when it was clear my body already had.

If her oldest child was ten a decade after she escaped to Canada, then the child couldn't have been her husband's. She was pregnant when she fled, as the medical records stated. Her husband was also Black. The boy's skin looked like mine. Which would mean that her baby's father was probably White. Only, in 1851 interracial relationships weren't allowed... Like a bungee jumper reaching the end of his slack, I felt everything snap into place with the realization that Mary must have been raped by her owner.

A quick google search confirmed my suspicions of how mixed children would have been treated after being discovered. The mixed children born into slavery were not accepted by their birth fathers. They were considered less-than for being mixed, and often rejected by both races. It felt uncomfortably familiar. Some of the women I read about had been accused by the owners of provoking the rape—as if such a thing were possible.

I thought of Chris and how he had kept saying it was just a misunderstanding between us. What would have happened to me if it had been 1851? I had read before that trauma could pass down from generation to generation through our DNA, and that never seemed as likely as right then. Maybe that was why I so quickly hid what had happened with Chris. Perhaps on some level I'd feared not being believed or being accused of having "provoked" it. And that's what everyone had said at Gibbons—that I had wanted it, asked for it.

Times hadn't changed at all, had they?

Steam was rising next to me, and I saw that at some point Ruby had placed a hot drink by my laptop and then retreated to sit quietly in one of the chairs nearby. Almost as if she was performing a vigil with me. Swallowing the lump in my throat, I looked more closely at the picture of Mary's family. Her oldest son was leaning back against his mother, and her arm surrounded him protectively. He was loved, I realized. Not ostracized or abandoned but loved. Mary's eyes looked haunted, yes, but they also looked fierce and alive even now, over a hundred years later.

It was as though some unknown force was driving me forward. I had never taken such an interest in history before, but it was *my* history this time. One of the links Jason sent had me going down a rabbit hole so deep I wasn't sure when or if I'd resurface. I followed family lines that were part of my ancestry, from Maryland into Canada in the 1850s. One of his—my, I guess—relatives had put the website together, and it was fascinating.

It seemed that once the escaped slaves—freedom seekers—made it into Canada, most congregated to a specific church in a city called Saint Catharines. Originally, they had met in a small log building that held about seventy people, but with the influx of freedom seekers into the city, they had needed a bigger building. I stumbled across an old photograph of the group who built the new church and nearly fell out of my chair when I saw Jason's last name listed. Mary's family had helped build the church. My heart swelled with pride. These were *my* people.

The building was formally designated a national historic site because it was "an important locus of abolitionist activity in Canada." *Wow.* That meant it was still there. I imagined myself standing in the same place where Mary had stood. I felt a connection to her greater than the one I felt with Jason, though I was sure that had more to do with the pain of being given away than anything else.

Suddenly I knew that this was what I had been waiting for. I could present my sociology project on my family's connection to Harriet Tubman and the Underground Railroad. The more I said it to myself, the more I liked it. *My family.* This would be right up

Professor Hawthorne's alley. It was the perfect combination of sociology and personal history. I was sure he'd love it.

Pulling out my phone, I typed Saint Catharines into my maps app. What I saw had me nearly bursting into our dorm room to shake Ruby—who had long since gone off to bed—awake. It was only a six-hour drive from NYC and, as though there were some magnetic pull compelling me, I knew that I had to go there.

7

It had taken some coordinating, but after borrowing Ruby's cousin's car, arranging for an official tour of the church because it was the only way to get in on a Saturday, and using some of my sacred savings from working at Brew to book a hotel for the night, we were on the road before dawn on Saturday. Our guided tour was at eleven a.m. sharp, and if we missed it, we were out of luck. The stern warning didn't seem very "Canadian" to me, but being at their mercy, I didn't bother arguing.

I took the first shift driving so that Ruby could get some more sleep. She had already cursed me more than once for forcing her out of bed so early, and I didn't want to take any chances.

Road trips always made me think of Lucas. I couldn't prevent my mind from drifting to him, wondering how he was doing, wondering if he was happy. Mela had respected my boundaries and hadn't mentioned him, but it wasn't like I had forgotten.

"What are you so focused on?" Ruby grumbled sleepily.

My eyes darted to her and back to the road. She was sitting up and rubbing her neck. "A past life." I smiled and then pulled off the highway to refuel and grab something with caffeine for both of us.

A few minutes later, Ruby was in the driver's seat, and I

gazed out the window, enjoying the blankets of snow atop the rolling hills around us. Old barns stood in fields of white, and it almost felt like going back in time a little.

There were questions I had always wanted to ask Ruby, but the timing had never seemed appropriate. Or maybe I had just been a chicken. I angled myself toward her and asked, "Were you ever…treated differently because of your skin color even though you're half White?" Holding my breath, I waited for her to answer. I wasn't stupid. I read the news. I knew people were treated differently, but I had never talked to anyone about it. Not anyone that looked like me anyway. Perhaps the topic was a bit heavy for this early in the morning, but I figured now was as good a time as any.

Ruby threw me a glance that questioned my intelligence but eventually answered me as though she had read my mind. "This is a pretty deep conversation for"—she glanced at her watch—"six a.m., but I'm going to hazard a guess that you've never been able to talk about it with anyone who looked like you."

I bit my lip and nodded as if making a terrible confession. The only person who looked like me had been the one in the mirror, and she had never had any answers. The words Ruby had spoken in class returned: *Damn, Liv. They, like, erased half your history.* I was beginning to realize that though it might not have been intentional, that was exactly what my adoptive parents had done.

"I've been bullied on both sides. Not Black enough to be Black, not White enough to be White. Neither side would claim me as a kid, and I used to wish I was just Black." She cut herself short and pursed her lips together.

"Used to?" I looked out the window again to give her some space in case she couldn't answer.

"I still do," she confessed, her voice barely above a whisper.

Feigning a yawn to cover the gasp that tried to sneak out, I supposed I couldn't really understand because I hadn't grown up with any people of color. Feeling that way was foreign to me.

I had never wanted to be one or the other; all I had wanted was simply to be accepted.

"What about you, Liv? What's the worst *you've* ever been treated for looking the way you do?"

I cringed, knowing the memory that would emerge in my mind before it even had a chance to register. Her knowing glance almost said *checkmate* to my question.

"I was ten." I bit the inside of my cheek to force myself to go on. "My parents put me into a summer program that happened at a local grade school I had never been to. The first day I became friends with a group of girls, and I couldn't wait to go back. But when I got to school the following day..." I blinked back the unexpected tears filling my eyes. *Still, Liv? Pull yourself together.*

Ruby focused on the road, but the way her hands gripped the steering wheel showed she was listening intently.

"The next day I ran up to the group, excited to play with them again, but I failed to notice the changed vibe. The leader, if you can call her that, turned to me and told me that they had decided there was only room for one Black girl in their group."

Ruby gasped. "No, she didn't!"

The shame came flooding back as though it were happening right there in the car. "I was confused because there were four White girls, one Black girl, and me. I was half and half and lived with a White family, ya know? But she turned to me and said, 'We chose her' and pointed to the Black girl. Then they turned their backs on me."

The silence in the car was deafening. I could taste blood on the inside of my cheek and made myself stop biting it.

"Liv...shit. I'm sorry, girl. What did you do?"

"I walked away. Pretended it didn't bother me." I shrugged even then, still trying to act like it hadn't scarred me.

"I would have punched her in the face." She looked over at me, and when our eyes met, it was as though an understanding had passed between us.

I smiled. "My violent streak didn't come until later."

She laughed as I told her about punching Katie Bryan in the face, but I still felt guilty about it.

"That's it? You know she deserved it. You shouldn't feel bad about that."

"How did you—"

"It's written all over your face, Liv. Evidently, we had very different experiences growing up. I've been in more fights than I can even remember. Sometimes fighting is the best way to get your point across." She raised an eyebrow at me.

I grimaced in response. "I prefer words."

"Says the English major."

Her belly laugh made the darkness lift for a moment, before it descended on me again.

"It wasn't only White people who mistreated me, though," I mumbled as another experience came to mind.

"It never is when you look like us." She nodded me on.

"I was sharing my opinion online on an acquaintance's post about something that had happened and she—a woman of color—said that I wasn't qualified to have an opinion because I was adopted into a White family. She told me I couldn't identify with people of color because I wasn't Black enough to."

Ruby sighed heavily. "Liv, I wish I could say that these were isolated events, but I've had so many similar experiences. So have pretty much all my mixed friends. But don't let someone you hardly know get in your head and convince you that your opinion isn't valid. You have every damn right to take up space. We both do."

The last thing she said felt more directed at herself than at me, but I appreciated the sentiment. It made me sad to think of so many people like us going through these things, but it also somehow made me feel less alone. I turned to watch the sky lighten as the wispy clouds became tinged with pink and orange—my favorite color combination for sunrises. I loved sunrises; they lifted the veil from the night before and chased away any shadows still lurking. Beauty, peace, comfort, and new beginnings: Mornings were my favorite.

We spent the rest of the drive exchanging stories we had never told each other and laughing so hard our stomachs hurt. The border was a breeze since we both had passports, and before we knew it, we were pulling up to the church.

It was a gable-fronted stucco-clad building on a high foundation. Its entryway was set between two large pointed-arch windows and approached by a split staircase. A large cross was spaced perfectly above and between the windows. Overall, it was simplistic but that added to its charm for me.

We parked right out front, and I was immediately drawn to a plaque that stood before it.

"Salem Chapel, built 1855, was an important centre of 19th century abolitionist and civil rights activity in Canada. Harriet Tubman, the famous Underground Railroad 'conductor,' lived near here from 1851 to 1858 and is traditionally associated with Salem Chapel. Many of those aided to freedom became church members and put down roots in the local community."

"Wow," Ruby and I whispered in unison.

As I stepped onto the staircase, however, I was struck by my own lack of emotion. I was right where I had seen my great—however many times—grandmother Mary standing in the picture, and yet I didn't feel the connection I had expected.

Ruby appeared beside me. "Ready?"

Not even a little bit. We went in anyway.

8

The inside of the church was a decent size and had four regularly spaced windows on each side, allowing the sunlight to flood the space. Its shape was rectangular, which Rachel, the tour guide, informed us was typical of the design of the Underground Railroad-related churches during that time. The furnishing was simple and had original fittings that had survived for over a century, including the long, single-log walnut benches.

"The heritage value of this church resides in its exceptional associations with the anti-slavery movement and the early Underground Railroad Black community." Rachel took a lot of pride in the tours she gave, that much was obvious. I thought I'd be hanging on to her every word, but instead I found it hard to focus.

We headed down to the basement, where Rachel continued our history lesson. "As you can see, photographs and materials line the walls here, detailing the history of the local Black community, freedom seekers, the Underground Railroad and its conductor—the church's most celebrated member—Harriet Tubman."

She went on to describe more of the perilous journey Harriet

Tubman and the other slaves had experienced. It was horrible hearing about the atrocities the escaped slaves had been made to endure, but I was still missing that feeling of connection I assumed would come naturally.

"Okay, I think we can take a look around on our own," I interjected suddenly. "We have another appointment we're meant to keep."

Ruby threw me a what-the-heck-are-you-talking-about look, but I just nodded and smiled at Rachel as though I weren't lying through my teeth. I knew that whatever I was looking for wouldn't be in the tour or that church.

Once enough time had passed for us to extricate ourselves politely, we headed to the Tim Hortons down the street, where I sipped a French vanilla cappuccino and Ruby drank a dark roast coffee. I pulled out my phone and scoured all the information I had about Mary.

"Do you want to tell me what that was about back there?" Ruby said.

"You'll be the first to know when I figure that out," I replied without looking up.

"What are you looking for, exactly?"

"I'm not really sure; I'll know it when I find it."

Again her lips pursed, yet she kept quiet and let me scroll obsessively through my phone. I thought I heard her mumble something about my being *cryptic* but ignored it.

Suddenly I sat up straighter. "Didn't we pass by Stormont County on the way here?"

"Umm, maybe?" Ruby didn't seem too sure.

I checked the maps app on my phone and, sure enough, Stormont County was only a twenty-five-minute drive away.

"Are you gonna tell me what this is about?" I had practically dragged Ruby out of Tim Hortons, and I was already driving us to our new destination.

I nearly laughed at the confused expression on her face. "Sorry, Ruby. I'm not crazy, I swear."

"That's debatable."

"My many-times great-grandmother Mary lived in Stormont County, I think. I saw it mentioned in the attachments Jason sent me."

"Oh, okay. So, you're the new tour guide, huh?"

"Something like that."

We pulled into a quaint little town—the kind with planter boxes lining the sidewalks in the summertime and elderly couples moseying along from shop to shop. There were still a few people walking around outside, but February hadn't released its wintery grip yet, and everyone we saw was hastily making for the shelter of the shops. I parked on a side street. In the distance stood a small white church with a cross on the roof; as though my feet had a mind of their own, I found myself heading in that direction.

I pulled my jacket a little tighter around me and saw Ruby do the same as a cold breeze assaulted us. It felt chillier here than back in New York, possibly due to the giant lake I could see between street corners. We walked up to the church; the sign in front of it read, "Mount Zion African Methodist Episcopal Church and Mount Zion Cemetery". Knowing it was a church predominantly for Africans, I wondered if Mary had spent any time there.

We walked up the steps and I tried to open the door, but it was locked. Ruby was stamping her feet on the ground and rubbing her hands together quickly as she tried to warm them with her breath. *Maybe I should just give up,* I thought glumly.

Deciding to take one last chance, I walked around the side of the church and to the cemetery in the back. The gravestones were spaced out randomly and quite far from each other. They were different shapes and sizes, and some looked ancient. Silently, Ruby and I split up and began to wander through the cemetery. I studied every one of the tombs, looking for the last name Pritchard, and when I saw a cluster of graves together, I moved in that direction. As soon I got up to one of the largest ones, I froze in my tracks.

Mary Pritchard, loving wife, mother, and grandmother. 1834 - 1935

The headstone was rectangular in shape and seemed to be made of a bluish gray stone with the words etched into it. Gently I placed my hand on top of it and let it rest there for a moment as I collected myself. On the headstones surrounding her grave I noticed the names of the children that I had seen in the picture of Mary with her family.

Jason Pritchard, 1851 - 1943, Robert Pritchard, 1853 - 1948, Maria Statton, 1857 - 1949, John Pritchard, 1854 - 1953

I wondered when her eldest son would have changed his last name to Pritchard. It made sense, I wouldn't have wanted my rapist father's last name either.

I moved to take a closer look and let my fingers run along each headstone as I passed by, almost like I didn't want to leave anyone out. Beyond Mary's immediate children, I found more headstones with the name Pritchard and surmised by the dates of life and death that they were likely her grandchildren. I touched each headstone, marveling at how much family surrounded Mary's grave.

Perhaps this was the dream life she had imagined for herself as she braved the perilous journey from slavery to freedom while pregnant. I couldn't fathom the kind of courage that would have taken. The kind of fortitude she must have had to decide that a life of slavery was not how her story would play out or end. To escape knowing that she might die or, worse, be recaptured and tortured for her defiance. To risk everything and secure a better life for herself, and a future free of slavery for her children and grandchildren, and…me.

A sob burst out of me as though the pressure had become too much to contain. But they weren't tears of grief. They were—and I was surprised to realize it—a mixture of relief and joy. "I came from courage," I whispered to myself. Mary had lived a long, beautiful life, over a century, surrounded by her husband, children, and grandchildren. Everything she went through had been worth it. And when she came to Canada, she dedicated her life to helping other freedom seekers who came after her to heal.

I thought of the brave yet wounded girls from the support group and felt a new resolve to help not only them, but all women who had ever gone through something so horrific. My experiences would serve to stand up for others. To stand in the gap for those who had no voice.

My tears had dried, and I felt more at peace with myself. I knew I wouldn't be able to make a difference for everyone, but I also believed that I would be able to make a difference for *someone.* And that that someone was worth fighting for.

I caught Ruby's eye. She nodded with understanding, as though she knew all the conclusions I had just come to. Only a few minutes had passed, but it felt as if a lifetime of grief, joy, relief, and hope had gone through me. As if I had previously been untethered and now I had an anchor in Mary.

Now I was grateful that Jason had sent me the information that had led me to her. No longer would I feel around in the dark for who I was. I knew who—and what—I came from, and the rest, as they say, would be up to me.

9

The next few days back in NYC were a bit of a blur. Between intensified track practices to prepare for the meet, my sociology project, and volunteering for Soul Care, I was running out of stamina.

"Olivia?" I jumped at the male voice. Ben Packer was running beside me and, by the look on his face, he'd been trying to talk to me for a while.

"Sorry, what was that?" I wasn't sure how many laps I had run. *Was it three or four?*

"I said, when was the last time you had a good night of sleep?" His gray eyes were full of concern.

Yikes, was it that obvious?

"Sleep? What's that?" I meant to say it with a laugh, but it came out too forced to be believable.

"You can only do so much, you know."

His voice was soft, but his words filled me with frustration. I wanted to punch something, but instead I shook out my hands.

"I'm fine, Ben. Honestly. I have a lot of cool things I'm working on, and I guess I just need to learn how to prioritize my time." I smiled at him, knowing he was just trying to help.

"Or delegate. My offer still stands, okay?" With his words left hanging in the air, he picked up the pace and left me alone with my thoughts.

He had offered to help with different things a few times, but he had also asked me out more than once, and I didn't want to accept his help and feel like I owed him something. I wasn't ready to move on from Lucas. I didn't know if I ever would be, despite all the reasons for us to end things. Or rather, for *me* to end things.

Once I finished my cool down and waved at a few friends, I decided to run back to my room to shower. I was a bit late and wanted to get to the support group room as soon as possible. I wanted to get a few things done for Professor Powell before anyone else got there. She had given me a key to the room so that I could send emails and make calls from the office.

I showered in record time and hurried to the room. Between rushing and being so distracted, I nearly missed it: Someone was sitting to the right of the door with her head between her knees. I slammed on the brakes when I saw that it was Lucy. Long dark hair, soft porcelain skin, ripped jeans. We'd sat beside each other every week but had never had an actual conversation.

"Lucy?" I approached cautiously.

When she looked up, I stifled a gasp. To say she had been crying would have been an understatement. Her normally striking blue eyes were so bloodshot I was surprised her tears weren't actual blood, and her cheeks were bright red, blotchy, and tear soaked. It was hard to resist the urge to throw my arms around her. *Not your usual inclination, you big softie.*

Sliding to the ground beside her, I let the silence between us stretch to such an uncomfortable point that I finally had to break it. "Wanna talk?"

She sniffed in response. My cheeks burned with shame at not knowing what to do or how to help. *If you're going to do this for a living, you'd better figure this out.* Getting to my feet, I turned and unlocked the door.

"Why don't you come in and have some tea?" Who knew if she liked tea, but it was all we had.

"Got anything stronger?" she croaked. We smiled at each other, and it eased the tension.

"Unfortunately not. But a cup of tea and a friend can sometimes be as good as a stiff drink." It was along the lines of something I had heard my mom say once; I doubted she'd said anything about a stiff drink, but I was improvising.

Lucy smiled shyly and took the seat I offered. Discreetly I pushed a box of tissues toward her and busied myself with the tea so she could collect herself. When I saw that she was calm enough to talk, I placed the mug in front of her and sat on the opposite side of the desk, waiting.

"You guys are the only ones who know that I was attacked by my ex-boyfriend," she began.

Nodding with understanding, I encouraged her to go on.

"I never reported it or told my parents. All I wanted was to forget about it, you know?"

I did know. Much more than she realized.

"Anyway, a friend from back home told me that he was just arrested for—" A sob escaped and drowned out the words she was trying to get out.

The back of my neck tingled as if someone were watching me, but I knew no one would be there. I knew my body was just reacting to what she was about to tell me. And I also knew that it was going to be terrible. My hands gripped the arms of my chair below the desk as I prepared myself.

But nothing could have prepared me.

"The woman he attacked wasn't even his girlfriend. She was —is—a mom. Married, even. She's been in a coma for three weeks. They say she may not ever wake up again…" She buried her face in her hands and wept.

I sat frozen in my seat and could feel how wide open my eyes were. While trying to control my face, I slowly stood up and moved to sit next to her.

She's in a coma—won't ever wake up again.

She's in a coma—won't ever wake up again.

She's in a coma—won't ever wake up again.

The words kept replaying in my mind like a CD skipping. The amount of trauma she would have had to endure to possibly never regain consciousness—my mind couldn't comprehend it. My breath came out in ragged gasps, and I forced myself to control it the way I would on the track. In through the nose, out through the mouth. As soon as I had a grip on my breathing, I placed my hand on Lucy's arm and she jerked it away.

"Don't. Don't touch me," she mumbled.

"I'm sorry," I whispered, wishing that someone with more experience would come in and know what to do. But I was all she had, so I refused to run.

"I don't deserve any compassion." Her voice sounded bitter, and it confused me.

"Lucy, you're as much a victim as anyone else," I repeated the words Professor Powell had spoken to me a few weeks before and hoped they would have some kind of effect.

"If I had just said something. If I had reported him, he wouldn't have been able to do this. She's hurt because of my inaction, and I'll have to live with that for the rest of my life. I'll never be able to make this right. I'm a damn coward!" She yanked some more tissues out of the box and aggressively wiped her eyes and nose.

I winced as the blotches on her face grew a deeper shade of red. "Lucy, I—"

She looked at me expectantly, but I trailed off. I didn't know what to say to make her feel any better. *What if I'm the reason Chris was able to hurt more girls?* Assuming that his other victims had been attacked before me was a mistake. As I watched Lucy sink behind a wall of despair, it became clear that my assumption was foolish. They could have easily been hurt after me, and I should feel as guilty as Lucy. I hadn't reported him—not officially anyway. So, I said nothing. What right did I have to? Instead, I just sat beside her until she ran out of tears.

Later, in the solitude of my dorm room, I sat on my bed turning my phone over and over again, thinking about everything that had happened with Lucy. How her ex-boyfriend was just like mine, and how there were likely a million other guys just like them. I dialed the number I had unintentionally memorized by looking at it so often.

"Officer Schmidt? It's Olivia Jackson. Yes, I have thought about it. I'd very much like to testify against Chris."

When the call ended, I cried myself to sleep.

10

Two weeks were left until I flew back to Florida. I had run out of time by taking so long to decide. I knew I had nothing to feel ashamed about, but I was getting nervous nonetheless.

Ruby and I were obsessively watching old episodes of *Law & Order SVU* late into the night. My dream life didn't improve, but I hoped that it would prepare me for what might happen in court. Mela was thrilled I was going back to Florida and joining us for watch parties through FaceTime. It was a bit macabre, but she wanted to support me, and I loved her for it.

My every spare second was spent on research for my sociology project. I didn't know how long the trial was going to last, and I wasn't about to get back to New York unprepared.

"Very studious of you." Ruby nodded in approval as I scribbled some notes about what I had just read.

"Thanks." I knew her well enough now not to assume she was being sarcastic. She took education more seriously than anyone I had ever met.

We were sitting in the cafeteria for pasta night. I liked to carb up before a track meet, and since there was one the following day, it was my last chance. Unfortunately, I had just lost my appetite.

"What's up?" Ruby asked.

I sighed before reading aloud what I had just read. "Many slave women gave birth to mixed-race or what used to be called 'mulatto' children following sexual assaults at the hands of White men."

I pushed my plate away in disgust. Having already suspected that Mary was raped by her slave owner, I'd found confirmation. The number of women of color who had been assaulted was horrifying, and it was really starting to get to me.

"I hate that term," Ruby said quietly.

"What? Mulatto?" My parents had always referred to me as that whenever someone had asked about my heritage, and I had adopted the practice. "I thought it just meant mixed. Half White, half Black."

"That's *one* definition. The word may have originated from the Arabic term *muwallad*, which means in literal translation a person of mixed ancestry. It referred to a person born of parents of Arab Muslim and non-Arab Muslim people."

"Okay…that doesn't sound so bad." I wasn't following.

"That definition isn't. But it also meant young mule in old Portuguese," she answered, as though that was explanation enough.

I stared at her with a blank expression on my face.

"A mule is a hybrid of two different animals—a horse and a donkey. Hybrids were sterile and therefore useless. The term was adopted for mixed babies during the slavery era and used in a derogatory way. It's not exactly a compliment."

I stared. Surely my parents had no idea of the connotations associated with that word. How many times had I told people that I was mulatto? *Like an idiot.* My cheeks were ablaze with a mix of rage and humiliation. How could I have been so naive?

Sitting there, burning with frustration, I finally shoved my things into my bag, stood up and, without saying a word to

Ruby, I left. My mind was a million miles away, and I aimlessly wandered through the city for a long time. Eventually, I found myself walking along Bow Bridge in Central Park, watching the sky change colors. It had become one of my favorite spots in the city, so I was unsurprised that my feet had carried me there. I stopped at the halfway point of the bridge and rested my elbows on the railing as I looked out over the water.

Ruby understood what I was feeling, but she had also grown up knowing everything I was just now learning. What I should have always known. What I *would* have always known if I hadn't been adopted by a White family who made no effort to educate me on my own history. Maybe it wasn't fair to feel that way, but I was getting tired of the guilt that arose whenever I had a less than generous thought about my parents. A Black Barbie didn't exactly translate into, "By the way, your ancestors were likely sexually assaulted by their White owners resulting in mixed-breed babies who weren't accepted by society." It also wasn't lost on me that I, too, had been assaulted just like my ancestors—just like Mary.

On a whim, I sent a text to Jason before realizing it was after ten p.m. How long had I been on that bridge?

Can you talk?

I put the phone away, assuming he wouldn't answer—but then it buzzed in my pocket.

Of course. What's up?

I stared at the trees covered in snow around the pond and watched as my breath formed clouds of smoke in front of my face.

I am really struggling lately with the fact that my adoption completely erased the Black side of my heritage. To the point where I don't even know what it means to be Black because I feel like an imposter...if that makes sense.

I pressed send before I could change my mind. As usual, I only realized what I was feeling as I typed it out. I watched "delivered" turn to "read" under the message and then my phone went dark before he had even begun to respond. I wondered if he would. *What do you even say to that?* After a full five minutes, the phone vibrated in my hand.

Yes, it makes sense. I feel your frustration. My whole life I was neither Black completely, nor German/White, or Indigenous. I was commonly referred to as mixed. A lot of biracial people feel that disconnect. Especially if they don't really know the other side of their heritage. A lot of mixed babies were placed for adoption because of the remnants of the one-drop rule.

That sounded ominous.

Do I even want to know what that is?

He replied quickly.

Probably not. But it was historically believed that if someone had even one drop of African blood in their ancestry, then they were considered less-than. A lot of White women have given their babies away to avoid the drama of having been in an interracial relationship.

Mulatto. Right. I wondered if that was why Ali gave me away. My phone buzzed again.

Before you even consider it, no, that's not why Ali placed you for adoption. We weren't ready to be parents.

I nearly laughed. Ready or not, you *were* parents the moment I was conceived. Deciding to pick only one controversial subject at a time, I hit reply.

How did you feel growing up?

I realized that he might have felt even more lost than I had. At least I had a connection to half of my history. He would have had nothing at all.

For me, I hated being Black or deemed Black most of my life. It was like I was being punished for something I had no choice about. I was belittled by both sides. It wasn't until recently that I really came to terms with and embraced it.

I thought back to my experience at summer camp and the online conversation, and realized that I had felt it too. Being dismissed for the color of my skin or who I had been raised by was inexplicably painful.

How did you embrace it?

I bit my lip as I waited for his reply.

I had to come full circle with my heritage to fill the emptiness inside myself. When I got to the other side, I realized that it wasn't, nor had it ever been, about race. It was about accepting all the parts that make me who I am. That's where I found peace and healing.

I traced a design in the fresh snow that had fallen on the railing beside me. It sounded simplistic, but I knew the journey there would have been difficult.

Thank you, Dad.

It was the first time I had ever referred to him as that, and it felt weird and kind of like I was betraying my adoptive dad. But I knew that Jason was trying, despite not having looked for me, and I also knew that I needed to let that go. I understood him on a much deeper level now, and felt connected to him in a way I hadn't felt before.

Anytime, baby girl.

I smiled at his term of endearment, knowing that we had just reached a new chapter of our relationship.

11

"Olivia Jackson in first..."

The announcer was calling the results of the 200-meter race that I had just crushed.

I returned the high five my teammate Pascale had just given me and smiled as Alyssa linked her arm through mine.

"What were you thinking about during that race, girl? You looked positively menacing." Her dark curls shook as she giggled.

"You wouldn't believe me if I told you." *Oh, you know, the usual—my people being oppressed and abused and letting that rage consume me.* I would have laughed, but I wasn't in the mood.

I felt better after my talk with Jason the night before, but I was still so frustrated by the atrocities I had been researching. None of it was fair, and I felt helpless to change anything.

My next event was the long jump, and I was going to be late if I didn't hurry. We were on the largest indoor track I had ever seen, and the fact that they had bleachers inside was impressive. Coach Grant gave me an enthusiastic thumbs up as I passed, and I gave her a quick smile in return.

I checked in for the event and waited until it was my turn. More than a dozen college track teams were there, but for once I wasn't preoccupied with sizing up the competition. I was there to win, and it didn't matter who I was competing against.

When they called my name, I stepped onto the track to prepare. As I stared down the straightaway to get lined up for my jump, the memory of running from Chris after he attacked me went through my mind. I jolted and shook my head to clear it. Even now, years later, it filled me with rage to remember how afraid I'd been. I let the anger fuel my jump as I hit the board and soared through the air.

I grabbed my ribbon after the event and took my time walking back to my team. Even though I had won every event so far, the usual butterflies of excitement in my stomach were missing. Instead, I felt anger. It was so distracting that I hadn't even let myself think about the fact that I would fly to Florida in a few days. I could only do one thing at a time, and right then it was simply to run.

The 100-meter final was next on the track, so I finished stretching and headed over to the starting line. Adjusting my blocks to the perfect spacing, I took a few practice starts to ensure they were right. Satisfied, I bounced up and down on the balls of my feet to stay warm before the race started. Sporting the black and red Carleton track uniform, I stepped into the blocks as the announcer called us to take our mark.

"Get set."

The gunshot went off.

The race seemed to finish before it started, and I could hardly remember pounding down the track at top speed. If I hadn't been holding another first-place ribbon, I might not believe the race had even happened.

"You keep running like this and no one will ever be able to catch you, Olivia." Pascale tapped my shoulder playfully as she passed me. *That's the idea.* I was just ensuring that my scholarship would be safe. I loved running, but more important things had taken center stage in my life lately. My parents still could not pay for my college, so I was grateful for the chance to keep attending with minimal costs.

The last event was the 4x100-meter relay, and I was anchoring it, as promised by Coach Grant. Amy Hamilton would start us off and hand the baton to Alyssa, who would hand it to Pascale, and finally she'd hand it to me and I'd run down the straightaway to the finish line. We were all in position, bouncing up and down. As I watched Amy step into the starting blocks, the track suddenly transformed in my mind and my teammates disappeared, replaced by my ancestors. I imagined Mary was starting out the race the way she had bravely leapt to freedom. As she ran around the bend of the first hundred meters, I imagined her whole life going by, and then her passing the baton to her children.

Alyssa took the baton from Amy and flew down the straightaway, and it was as if I were watching two versions of the same race. In the second version, Mary's children were living in freedom and having their own children and grandchildren. Slavery was abolished, and they were free to immigrate back to the United States. And then, as Alyssa passed the baton to Pascale and she leaned into the bend to bring it to me, I imagined it was Jason overcoming all obstacles to get well enough and be in my life.

I turned and prepared myself for Pascale's signal for me to take off. The moment I heard her yell, "Go," I ran. As I reached my left arm back to grab the baton from her, I was overcome with the sense that I was being passed the baton in more ways than one. It was my turn to run this race, and my race. My teammates had done all they could to get me to that point, just as my ancestors had. It was up to me to finish as strongly as I could, and so I ran with everything I had, leaving it all on the track.

Afterwards, I ran a light lap to cool down. With the track meet behind me, I had nothing left to do but focus on my trip to Florida and everything I would have to face. Suddenly I had to fight a little harder to take a deep breath. The last time I was home remained fresh in my mind: the way Lucas had come to my track meet to see me win and then disappeared before I could say goodbye. How hurt Mela had seemed when she found out I'd be leaving. My determination to become a completely different person—and yet, I still felt like the same old me.

I had never thought I'd have to face Chris in court, but I was glad to be adding my voice to those of the other witnesses. He had gotten away with too much already, and if there was a chance that we could get him put in jail...perhaps that would be the vindication I had been looking for. I could not erase the past, but I had an opportunity that my ancestors—that Mary—never had. I would stand up in court and say that what happened to me was evil. The women of the past had had to run away from their abusers; in some small way, I was standing in the gap for them. I would have the chance to be heard, to be listened to, and that is something they'd never had.

When I stepped off the track, I knew that, ready or not, I'd be back in Florida very soon. But I didn't know what would be waiting for me there.

12

"Ladies and gentlemen, we have begun our descent into Fort Lauderdale. Please turn off all portable electronic devices and stow them until we have arrived at the gate. In preparation for landing, make sure your seat is in the upright position and your seatbelt is fastened."

The captain's voice sounded like a whisper, as my ears hadn't yet popped.

I leaned back in my window seat and stared out at the ocean. Bits of yellow and white hugged the water at the shore, and it still amazed me that those little lines were vast expanses of sand. The sun danced on top of the water, and my body hummed with longing at the sight. Now that I saw it again after so many months, I knew that the sun sparkling on the ocean beat the snow any day of the week. There was truly no comparison.

As the pressure in my ears got painful, I shifted uncomfortably in my seat. Giving up, I pinched my nose shut and gently blew until I heard the release of air that signaled my ears had popped. The plane was suddenly much louder than it had been a few moments before. The engine drowned out nearly everything else, but I could still hear pockets of conversations, overly loud laughter from the ladies a few rows over who hadn't cleared their ears yet, and the movie blasting through the headphones of the guy next to me.

Before I knew it, we were taxiing along the runway and pulling up to the gate. I smiled to myself as everyone stood the moment the seatbelt sign was turned off. It never failed to make me chuckle. Where did they think they were going? The doors wouldn't open for several minutes, but everyone lined up like they were in a race to get to the front. A few other passengers stayed seated with knowing smirks on their faces.

The sensation was fleeting as the reason for me to return sank in. This wasn't a social visit. My fingers fidgeted with the straps on my backpack as I waited. Anxiety spread through my body like a disease taking over healthy cells. By the time I was walking through the airport, I had become a ball of nerves. I kept my head down to avoid anyone's eyes as I headed to grab my luggage.

As soon as I was halfway down the escalator, I heard my name being called. I searched the crowd and found Mela waving so enthusiastically I thought her arm might fall off. I smiled despite myself. She looked great in a white crop top and skinny jeans. Her hair was thrown up expertly into a messy bun, sunglasses perched on her head. She was practically bouncing with excitement and flung her arms around me the second I stepped off the escalator. I squeezed her back and breathed in her familiar perfume.

She finally pulled back and said, "Hi." It made us burst into laughter. "You look great! Your hair is…wowza," she added as she linked her arm through mine and led me to the baggage claim.

I looked down at my ripped jeans and Carleton hoodie, knowing that the dark circles under my eyes were much more prominent than usual, but I had styled my hair curly for the occasion. Still, I wasn't sure "great" was the best description.

"Great considering what you're back here for. Better?"

We both knew I looked exhausted, but I loved her for not saying it.

Once I had collected my suitcase, ripped off my sweater because, Florida, and settled into Mela's SUV, we were on the road.

"When did you get this?" I gestured to the vehicle.

"Last week. I think my dad feels guilty for working so much. And he should."

I raised my eyebrows in response to her tone. His not being around wasn't a surprise to me; it had kind of always been that way. It seemed like there was more to it than she was saying, and I made a mental note to ask her about it later.

"So, where to? My place to avoid the inevitable awkward conversation? Or to your parents' place to get it over with?" She flashed me her best both-options-suck smile and I grimaced in response.

"I may as well get it over with; they're expecting me anyway."

Way too soon, we pulled into my parents' driveway and I hopped out with my luggage in tow.

The house looked exactly as when I'd left. For some reason, that fact surprised me as though I had expected some major changes. I supposed they were empty nesters now, so they could do what they wanted—which apparently was nothing.

At the door, I hesitated. Normally, I would have walked right in, but somehow it didn't feel right. I didn't live there anymore. I knocked lightly on the door and waited. After a minute, heavy footsteps approached and the door opened to reveal my dad, whose blue eyes were crinkled in confusion.

"Why are you knocking? Get in here, you little rat." He pulled me into a crushing hug, burying my face in his stomach, and my defenses melted away. The familiar smell of Old Spice and some knock-off deodorant swirled through the air, and suddenly I felt like a child climbing into her daddy's lap after having been at a sleepover.

"Hey, Dad," I mumbled into his black t-shirt as he still hugged me too tightly.

He gave me one last squeeze before releasing me and carrying my suitcase into the house.

It smelled like pasta sauce, and I smiled, knowing that my mom was probably cooking way too much so she could freeze a bunch. Sure enough, when I walked into the kitchen plastic containers of all shapes and sizes lined the counter. From old cottage-cheese tubs to actual name brand Tupperware, they were all filled with sauce, waiting to be closed up and moved into the deep freeze.

My mom was at the stove, stirring something in a big pot with her back to me. The same old apron with its frayed fabric was hanging around her thin waist. Her hair had much more gray than the last time I had seen her.

She turned to me and wiped her hands on her apron before pulling me into a long hug. I let myself settle into it, knowing that I was about to drop yet another bomb on them, and tried to hold on_to the moment for as long as I could.

"I missed you, honey. Your hair looks fantastic. How did you get it so curly?" She smiled warmly and turned back to her bubbling pot of pasta sauce.

"My roommate helped." There were other things I wanted to say but I left it at that.

The memory of my dad standing in front of her protectively, accusing me of hurting her, flashed across my mind and made me wince. I stood in almost the same spot as then. Would it go the same way? I wondered. *It's going to be fine.*

We exchanged small talk for a while and then shuffled into the living room. I didn't miss the look my parents exchanged when they thought I couldn't see them. Almost as soon as I sat down on the multi-colored couch they had gotten at a garage sale, they were on me.

"So, what is this about, Liv? What couldn't wait until the end of your semester?" My dad looked anxious but hopeful that I was about to say something better than what he'd imagined. I feared I would greatly disappoint him.

"Do you remember Chris?" I started carefully. Their blank stares caused me to continue my explanation. "We dated for a few months a couple of years ago. He was older…" I was getting nowhere and began to realize just how checked out my parents had been then.

"It's not ringing a bell." My mom was trying to piece it together.

I sighed in response. "He used to pick me up in his Camaro with the loud music playing all the time."

My dad's eyes brightened in recognition. "Oh yeah, that guy. I remember now."

I pulled at the rip in my jeans, willing it to get me through the rest of the conversation. "Okay, so one night he tried to force —" I choked on the words but made myself continue. "He tried to force himself on me. It was—it was really scary." My eyes welled up with tears at the memory of trying to push him off, knowing I wouldn't be able to.

"What did he do? Did he—" My mom couldn't even finish the sentence.

"No. No, he didn't," I mumbled.

"Where were you when it happened?" Her eyes were full of concern.

I hated to admit it, but it was so long ago—no sense in lying about it. "I was at his apartment."

I hadn't had permission to go to his place.

"*Alone?*" Her eyes were wide. "Olivia, I've told you so many times you should never be alone with a guy like that. Especially then, at that age." Her frustration was spilling over, and I couldn't blame her.

"I know, Mom. Believe me, I wish I could change what happened. It's not like I wanted to go there. He didn't give me much of a choice."

"There is always a choice, honey."

"Right. Well, I tried to forget about it and move on, but then he started following me and waiting for me after work." I kept my eyes glued to the carpet. *Has the green in it always looked so faded?*

"What did he *do*?" my dad demanded, repeating my mom's question.

"He didn't—I mean, he tried to." Words were failing me spectacularly. "His roommate stopped him," I finally blurted out.

"Why didn't you come to us?" His tone pleaded with me.

I swallowed hard. "I wanted to, I did. But it felt like a problem I had caused. I thought I could deal with it myself." My eyes darted to my mom's face then straight back to the carpet.

"You could have been seriously hurt, Olivia." It came out like an accusation, but she was just scared.

"I know, Mom." I sighed again before going on. "Anyway, Lucas found Chris waiting for me after work one day and they got into a fist fight." It hadn't been much of a fight, really. Lucas had beaten the crap out of Chris.

"Good." My dad was smiling in a way I had never seen before. The temperature in the room seemed to drop by several degrees.

"Yeah, well, it wasn't so good, actually. Lucas got arrested and I tried to convince the police not to press charges, but without any proof that Chris had hurt me, there was nothing they could do."

"You went to the police station? Why didn't they call us?" The look of disbelief on my dad's face was almost comical, but a laugh at that moment would have gone over about as well as a grenade.

"I don't know, Dad. But I ended up going to the hospital and tricking Chris into admitting what he did and threatening to release the recording if he pressed charges against Lucas." My shoulders sank with relief. *There. That's everything.*

"The *hospital*? I knew Lucas was bad news," my mom said.

"Lucas?" My dad and I said it simultaneously. She merely crossed her arms.

"Anne, I think your anger is a bit misplaced here." My dad was trying to reason with her.

"Seriously, Mom. It was not his fault at all. He was protecting me."

"If that were true, then he would have come to your father and me. Instead, you both kept it a secret, and he took the law into his own hands. He put a man in the hospital. How are we supposed to protect you if you keep these things from us?" She wrung her hands, and the vein in her neck—the one that only made an appearance when she was incredibly upset—was in full view.

"I'm sorry, Mom. I really am. But I did what I thought was right at the time."

"But you didn't report Chris to protect Lucas, right? Do you really think that was the *right* call?"

"I wasn't about to let Lucas rot in jail. Was it the right call? Probably not. But it's the call I made." She wasn't making this easy, but she couldn't know how guilty I felt about staying quiet all this time.

"So why are you back now, honey?" My dad's face was the one he made when he wasn't quite connecting all the dots.

I figured there was no sense in beating around the bush. "Chris is being prosecuted, and I've been asked to testify against him."

"Olivia! Your inaction allowed him to attack *other* girls as well? You should have come to us." Mom was red in the face, and the vein was dangerously close to bulging.

"Anne." Her name escaped my dad's teeth through a hiss. His eyes were wide with shock as her accusation sucked the air out of the room.

I sat motionless in stunned silence as she stood up and left the room without saying another word.

Awkwardness dragged on between me and my dad until he

eventually broke it. "I'm sorry you didn't feel that you could trust us with this before, kiddo."

We stood, the conflict brewing beneath the surface of his gaze.

"It's okay, Dad. But, umm, I think I'll stay at Mela's. She offered and, uh, I think she's kind of lonely." I moved towards my luggage, still in the front hallway.

His face was a mixture of relief and frustration. "She just needs some time, Liv. This is quite a shock. Text me with any updates, okay?"

I nodded, not trusting myself to speak. Stepping outside, I looked back as I closed the door. A million memories were held in that house, but as I turned and walked away, I knew deep down that—for now, at least—it didn't feel like home anymore.

13

"You willingly went to his apartment alone, didn't you?"

"Well, yeah, I mean he was my boyfriend," I stammered as I shifted in my seat.

"What were you wearing that night?"

"Excuse me? Why would that matter?" *Breathe, Liv. You need to calm down.*

"Did you even ask him to stop?" The smirk on his face made me want to punch him in the mouth.

"How *dare* you! Of course I told him to stop. It's pretty hard to be understood with his damn hand over my mouth!" I squeezed my trembling fingers together to stop them from shaking.

"Let's stop for a moment." District Attorney Johnson's soft brown eyes gazed at me compassionately.

I threw a glare at the other lawyer, Gunner, and swiveled my chair away from him. The trembling in my hands hadn't subsided yet, so I kept them hidden under the cherry wood oval conference room table. A plaque with the state attorney's seal was fixed on the white wall across from where I was sitting. The obligatory diplomas, the photo with the partners smiling widely, and the heavy leather books were all there, as if to reassure clients. Pot lights right above us turned the lawyers' inquiring eyes silver and exposed me like the proverbial interrogation bulb would.

Gunner was still standing, but I refused to look over at him and instead fixed my eyes on Johnson, whose first name I couldn't remember, because she was the nicer of the two. She was wearing dark slacks and a yellow blouse that looked great against her tanned skin.

"You can expect this and much more, Miss Jackson." The sound of his voice behind me made me flinch.

His expression to Johnson was slightly exasperated, as if he didn't think I'd be able to do this. *He might be right.* He had loosened the tie on his black suit some time ago, and it made him appear slightly disheveled.

Johnson sat down beside me. "How are you feeling, Olivia? Here, have some water." She handed me a water bottle she had gotten from a small fridge in the corner. I held it with both hands and took a small sip.

"I'm fine." My voice was hoarse; I wasn't fooling anyone. How could victims be treated that way? We'd been at this line of questioning for forty-five minutes, and I was fighting the urge to cry.

"Mr. Jamieson's legal team is known for their…" Johnson trailed off, trying to think of the right word.

"Brutality?" Gunner offered much more pleasantly than the situation warranted. She pursed her lips at him.

"As I was saying, his legal team is pretty ruthless, so we need to get you as prepared as possible."

I thought I had known what I was in for, but no amount of *Law & Order* reruns could have prepared me for this. It wasn't going to be as simple as telling the truth on the stand; I could see that now. Chris's legal team was going to try to make me seem like I had wanted to be attacked, and I just wasn't sure how well I'd handle that.

"How many others are there?" I tried to sound stronger.

"Victims? Five." Forcing myself to look at Gunner as he answered, I nodded. He added, "I've been trying to find Chris's old roommate, Danny, but I haven't been able to track him down yet."

"Officer Schmidt said that Chris was being charged with aggravated sexual battery. What does that mean?" I directed the question at Gunner, reminding myself that he was on my side.

"Let's just say that you got off easy compared to some of the others."

I shuddered. "He also said that Chris was facing at least nine years in prison if convicted. That seems like a lot, considering that two years ago they told me it was hard to actually put guys like him behind bars."

"It's because you were all under eighteen at the time of your assault." Johnson's tone was warm, but it felt like I had been plunged into an icy river.

"*All* of us?" He had made me feel so special. Made me believe that he didn't mind my age only because I was different, when in truth he was a predator. *How could I have fallen for such a creep?*

"It's a lot to take in, I'm sure. But the point is that it's been two years now, and they're going to drill you on why you didn't report him." Gunner's tone had softened but I was still frustrated.

"I told you why already." I hadn't been willing to let Lucas rot in jail.

"About that…" They exchanged another glance, one that told me I wasn't going to like whatever came out next.

"About what?" I demanded.

Johnson put her hand on my arm. "Chris's defense team has subpoenaed Lucas. He'll have to testify."

"No! Absolutely not. They can't!" The tears I had been holding back for an hour threatened to spill over.

"They can and they have." Gunner adopted a sympathetic tone, but I was still wary of him after his line of questioning.

"Why, though?"

"My guess is they want to discredit you. Of course, we have no way of knowing—but if it were me, I'd want to call Lucas's character into question and show the jury that he is a violent and impulsive guy who hurt a very innocent Chris."

"Oh, please," I spat.

"Their angle is likely going to be that you are a wild girl who consorts with trailer-trash," Johnson said. "That you hatched a plan with your boyfriend Lucas to get Chris's money and involve him in other schemes. They'll want to destroy your reputation by destroying Lucas too. The Jamieson family has hired private investigators."

"What for?" I asked. But I already knew. She'd said they were going to try to discredit us; private investigators would make that easier.

My water bottle was shaking so badly that the water wouldn't stop sloshing around as I tried to drink. Memories of following Lucas to his mom's trailer that day swirled through my mind. *I'm trash, Liv. I come from trash.* That's what he had said. And now he was going to have his life picked apart in a room full of people, and it was all my fault.

"Olivia?" Someone was calling my name, but I couldn't make out who it was. The room was decidedly smaller than it had been a minute ago.

"Olivia?"

Is it hot in here? I pulled at the collar of my white t-shirt.

"Olivia, are you game for another role play involving this new line of questioning?"

I could hardly hear Johnson's words.

"I'm sorry, what did you say?" A ray of light with dust particles floating through it fell on a piece of paper on the table, and I wondered if it would light the paper on fire. Wouldn't it need a magnifying glass for that? I thought it might.

SNAP! Gunner's fingers snapped together in my face. I looked into his concerned dark eyes. *Pull it together, Liv.*

"There you are. Can you do this?" He sounded much softer now than when pretending to be the defense lawyer.

"No. Not today anyway. Can we meet tomorrow?" Spots were dancing in my vision, and I was afraid I might pass out if I didn't leave soon.

Gunner opened his mouth to argue, but Johnson shook her head at him. "That's fine, Olivia. We'll see you at nine a.m., okay?"

I nodded, not trusting myself to speak, and practically ran to my car. I pulled out my phone and typed a text to Lucas.

Can we talk?

I forced the air in through my nose and out through my mouth. Watching my stomach expand and contract with every breath began to calm me down. I blew out my breath and tried calling him instead because he wasn't answering my text fast enough.

"I'm sorry. The number you have dialed is not in service at this time. Please try your call again. This is a recording."

Disconnected? Reality hit me like a ton of bricks: All this time I had believed that he was just a text away. That someday we'd find our way back to each other, even if just as friends.

The truth hurt. We weren't in each other's lives, and I didn't even have his number anymore. But I did know who would.

14

For the first time in what felt like forever, I stood outside the Martin house. The door opened and Nate stood on the other side with a wide smile. He was in black shorts and a blue T-shirt, his blond hair ruffled as usual. He lifted me into a bear hug.

"Nate!" I laughed as he put me down.

"Took you long enough to come by," he said gently.

"I know, I know." I looked past him nervously and he answered my silent question.

"He's not here. He moved out a few months ago."

I couldn't hide my surprise. Lucas had seemed to really like living at Nate's. Nodding more to myself than to him, I walked into the living room and sat on the couch beside Mela, who hadn't bothered to get up. She was in the corner of the sectional, crocheting something that looked like a turtle.

"You crochet now?" It felt like I didn't even know my best friend anymore.

"You're damn right I do. This is addictive." She flashed me a grin and leaned up to kiss Nate, who had just walked over.

"Do you have his new number?" I asked Nate. "I...umm...I need to talk to him."

Mela's head turned sharply to me. "What's going on?" She knew I wouldn't be asking for his number if it wasn't serious.

Picking up on her body language, Nate sat beside her, seeming to brace himself.

I brought them up to speed on what the lawyers had told me. Nate's eyes bulged and Mela let out a low whistle.

"It's not good, I know. He should be warned at least." I bit my lip as I watched them exchange nervous glances. It was the same look the lawyers had given to each other before they'd told me that Lucas was being subpoenaed. "What aren't you telling me?" I demanded. Having information withheld from me was getting old.

"Liv, it's just that...well...Lucas hasn't been in a good place for a while." Nate spoke while Mela gripped my hand hard enough to keep me from pulling it away, though I was trying.

"What does that mean?"

"He's been withdrawn," Nate started, but Mela interrupted him with a bitter laugh.

"To say the least. He quit the football team, moved out of Nate's to go live with his douchy brother downtown because he didn't want to be a 'charity case' anymore." She put the words in air quotes and went on, "And I'm pretty sure he's started day drinking." Putting down her crochet turtle, she folded her arms.

"Mela..." Nate's voice carried a warning.

"I'm not keeping his secrets anymore, babe." She gave him a look that seemed to say, "I dare you to question me," and he sighed and looked away.

"Why didn't you tell me sooner, Mel?" I asked, though I knew the answer.

"You told me that talking about him was off limits until you were ready. I didn't want to burden you with this." Her eyes held a thousand unspoken words, and the years of friendship between us translated them for me. Something major had happened.

"What happened?" My question was directed at Nate.

He looked at me as though weighing the pros and cons of telling me. Mela elbowed him in the ribs, and he relented.

"He went looking for his dad, and what he found wasn't good." This was cryptic and I didn't think he was going to elaborate, so I waved my hand to tell him to go on. He did. "At first it seemed like a good thing. His dad came over, hung out with us, was a real smooth talker, ya know? He even talked to Lucas about maybe moving in with him. Lucas was really pumped."

The dread that surrounded me was suffocating, and I froze as if I had just stepped into quicksand. A cold bead of sweat rolled down my back. Mela clutched her crochet needles as she sat motionless beside me.

"In the end, though, we found out his dad only turned up because he thought he could get some money out of him. When he found out that that wasn't going to happen, he bailed. Lucas moved out a week later."

My nails were sinking into the back of my wrist so sharply that Mela pried them off. I had told Lucas I would help him find his dad the way he had helped me. I was selfish by pushing him away and not keeping in touch. I hadn't been there for him, and that was hard to bear.

"The trial is going to make everything worse for Lucas," I whispered, realizing it was true as I spoke the words aloud.

"Yes, it most likely will." Nate's voice was strained with the burden of having experienced years of friendship with Lucas and not being able to protect him from this.

Our eyes met and I could see how conflicted he was. "Give me his number, Nate." Suspicion was rising in me.

"I can't, Liv. I promised him I wouldn't." He looked away.

There it was. Lucas didn't want my help. I knew I deserved that, but it still stung. The necklace he'd given me hung like a noose around my throat, preventing me from responding.

Eventually, I found my voice again. "Will you at least warn him?" I asked softly.

"Yeah, of course, Liv. I'm…sorry." Nate really looked it.

"No, it's okay, Nate. I get it. Tell him…" I didn't finish. There were a million things I wanted to say to Lucas, but I couldn't. Nate seemed to understand.

"I will."

Mela looked at me with so much pity in her eyes that I couldn't take it anymore. I excused myself and headed back to her place on my own.

LATER THAT NIGHT, as I listened to the sound of Mela snoring softly beside me, I finally let the tears fall. There was absolutely nothing I could do to prevent the pain and embarrassment Lucas was about to endure. If I had simply said no to Officer Schmidt, then Lucas wouldn't have been subpoenaed. Yet I wouldn't have been able to live with myself if I had refused to testify, though the knowledge that Lucas was going to suffer felt like a freight train bearing down on me. Instead of moving out of the way, I was simply staring at the bright lights, hoping the train would veer off course on its own. I knew it wouldn't; this train was coming for us, and we were all tied to the tracks.

15

Though my lungs burned and my legs felt wobbly, I kept running along the beach. I had a few days off from prepping for the trial as the lawyers ran the other victims through the gauntlet. Hopefully, they'd fare better than I had.

Eventually my legs gave out and I collapsed on the sand with frustration. I sat cross-legged and dug rocks out of the sand to whip into the sea. Too much had been lost to me. Half of my heritage, Lucas, G.G.… I whipped another rock into the water.

Splash - *None of this is fair. Mary didn't risk her life for me to just accept it all.*

Splash - *I shouldn't have let Ali take my great-grandmother away from me.*

Splash - *Maybe I can't do anything about Lucas, but I can damn well do something about G.G.*

Suddenly I was pulling out my phone and texting Ali before I could chicken out.

We need to talk. I know you're in town. Meet me at the diner on Broadway in an hour.

It was handy that she kept her social media public, and for once I didn't feel guilty about checking in on her. I looked at her accounts far less than I used to, but every now and then I couldn't resist the pull to peek.

My phone buzzed in my hand.

Okay. Meet you in an hour.

Part of me was surprised that she'd agreed, but I figured she knew that I knew where her vacation home was and might just show up. She wasn't wrong; this had gone on for long enough.

Racing back to Mela's, I took a quick shower and got to the diner a few minutes before our set meeting time. I ordered a latte and sat in a booth facing the door so I could see when she got there. Five minutes later, she pulled into the parking lot in a sleek black SUV. I watched her walk to the door in high heels and a dark green sleeveless jumpsuit that tied around the waist, with ruffled shoulders to accentuate her tanned arms. Her blond hair looked professionally blown out, and her clutch purse matched her shoes. She looked…beautiful; and tense.

As her heels clicked toward me, her expression was reserved and maybe a bit curious, but not angry. *Maybe we're making progress.* She slid into the seat across from me and, as our eyes connected, hers were guarded. *Maybe not, then.*

"Thank you for meeting me, Ali," I started.

"I figured you would just show up at my house if I didn't."

Swallowing back the laugh that nearly escaped, I nodded. "Probably."

"What is this about, Olivia?"

The waitress came over and she ordered a black coffee. I wasn't sure how she choked the stuff down, but the coffee drinkers in my life had always told me it was a lifeline for them, so maybe it was the same with Ali. Maybe she was more rattled than she looked.

"I met Jason." It hadn't been how I had intended to start the conversation, but I went with it.

She didn't mask her shock. "You found him then?" Her lips were pursed, and her shoulders stiffened. She stirred sweetener into her coffee in a nonchalant way, but her eyes darted around the diner as though she expected him to jump out and scare her.

"I did. He's nice. Not how you described him at all. But I suppose nineteen years is a long time for someone to have stayed the same." Taking a sip of my drink, I let her absorb the information I was dropping on her.

"Okay. Did you…did you tell him anything about…"

"No, Ali. I didn't tell him anything about you. He didn't ask either, if that makes you feel any better."

She looked visibly relieved. It made me sad to see how afraid she was of him.

"Was that all you wanted to tell me?" Her eyebrows creased with confusion the way mine always did.

"I wanted you to know that now that I've met both of you, I can see how much meaning I had looked for in each. Those were unfair expectations, and I guess I'd like to apologize."

Her jaw dropped and she stared at me for a few moments before recovering enough to take a sip of her coffee, but not enough to say anything. I took advantage of her silence.

"I don't look for meaning in either of you, and I don't even feel like I need to have a relationship with you. But I *have* come to love G.G., and I know that she loves me too. Continuing to separate us is unfair—to us both."

It was possibly the most honest I had ever been with her, but it felt different knowing that what I was saying was true. I didn't need her approval anymore.

"I'll consider it." Her eyebrows were raised, almost daring me to argue.

I shook my head sadly. "That's not good enough, Ali. I think you need to get over yourself and stop blocking my great-grandmother from having a friend. Letting me see her isn't going to affect or harm you in any way, but it will enrich her life and you know it."

The truth was it would enrich my life as well. My biological family members were few and far between, and I was tired of letting Ali call all the shots. Her eyes narrowed ever so slightly as she calculated her options.

"On one condition," she countered. "You stop all contact with Leah. She's too young, and I know you hate me. I'm afraid that you'll get Leah to hate me too."

Her nostrils flared ever so slightly, and I was surprised to realize that she actually believed I hated her and—even more surprising—that it bothered her.

"I don't hate you, Ali. I just wanted you to accept me as your own; I wanted to belong. But I've realized that I never needed that—not from you anyway. I needed to accept myself. Besides, I've seen what hatred does to a person, and I don't want to be that way. I wouldn't want that for my little sister. She's a happy kid, and I want it to stay that way." I smiled, thinking of Leah.

"Be that as it may, that's my offer." She crossed her arms, and I could hear her foot tapping below the table.

"You don't get it because you weren't given away, but asking me to abandon family isn't something I can allow. I'm an adoptee; we don't just abandon people—not without an insanely good reason. So, no, I won't agree to those terms, but you have my word that I won't try to turn Leah against you."

We faced each other without saying a thing. I had shown all my cards and waited for her response. She looked wary and, in that moment, I saw how afraid she'd always been. For all her money and bravado, she was still a scared sixteen-year-old girl worrying about being judged or not liked. It surprised me to realize that I actually felt sorry for her. *My, how the tables have turned.*

"Fine. I'll pop by Tuscan Gardens and add you back to the approved guest list." Her shoulders slumped a little in defeat, but she also had a new look in her eye. It looked a little like…respect.

"Great! Let's go together." I moved to stand up, not wanting to let her agree and then not actually do it.

She held her hand up to stop me. "I just gave in to two things you wanted. Now let me do this my way. I have given you my word."

"And I'm just supposed to, what? Trust it?" My tone dripped with doubt.

"You're going to have to. I know you don't know me very well, Olivia, but when I give my word, I follow through."

She was right. I didn't know her well. In fact, I didn't know her at all. But she had agreed to my terms, and it wasn't like I could hold her at gunpoint until she took me to see G.G. I had my doubts, but she had promised. I was simply going to have to trust that she meant what she'd said.

16

"You should eat something, Liv." Mela's gaze was full of concern as she sat across from me at her kitchen table.

The plate of food her dad had made me sat untouched. Even the smell was enough to make me gag, but I knew it wasn't the food making my stomach turn. In an hour we'd be sitting in a courtroom with the trial underway. My belly heaved, and I swallowed whatever had been trying to make its way back up. I settled on a sip of water instead.

"I know, but I'm afraid I'll puke if I do. Can't risk getting this outfit dirty." I looked down at the clothes we'd found in Mela's late mom's closet. Her dad had refused to get rid of anything, so her entire wardrobe was still upstairs. We had settled on high-waisted black slacks with a matching cropped blazer and a loose cream tank top underneath. I had drawn the line at pearls, though.

"It's true. My mom would roll over in her grave." Her milk-chocolate eyes watched for my inevitable reaction, and she was not disappointed as I gasped and lightly backhanded her arm.

"You're so morbid." I shook my head at her, but it was more out of reverence for the way she was handling herself after her mother's death than anything.

She shrugged. "It's how I deal."

Popping a last bite of sausage into her mouth, she scraped her chair against the floor as she stood up. I watched her toss frozen tropical fruit into the blender, add some protein powder, a banana, Greek yogurt, three squirts of liquid stevia, some water and blend it all. She poured the result into a to-go cup with a lid and straw and thrust it into my hand.

"If you're not gonna eat, you can at least sip on this. We don't want you passing out on the stand now, do we?" She had said it in jest, but the concern hadn't left her eyes.

I closed my hand around the cup gratefully and even took a few sips. Though it was my favorite kind of smoothie, it tasted like sawdust in my mouth. Or whatever I assume sawdust would taste like, having never actually tried it.

Twenty minutes later we were pulling into the courthouse parking lot. My parents were going to be there for moral support, but I dreaded them listening to all the gory details. My life was going to be on display for everyone to pick apart, yet I refused to back down. Letting Chris off the hook wasn't going to be a part of my story anymore.

The pain in my chest that had grown steadily for days began to suffocate me. Lucas didn't deserve to have his life put on display. and I hadn't even been able to tell him how sorry I was that it was going to happen.

"He'll be okay, Liv." Mela seemed to know what I was thinking and squeezed my arm affectionately.

We faced the large white pillars framing the doors to the courthouse and started up the steps together. After going through security, we walked to the assigned courtroom.

As soon as we turned the corner, it felt like I had just entered a tunnel. The sounds of people chatting, the high heels clicking against the terrazzo floor, the law clerk who dropped his folders full of papers—they were all muted when I saw *him*. As though I were on a moving platform, my feet carried me to the courtroom door, where Nate stood with

Lucas, and Mela had to practically run to keep up. There were differences in him, but like in a forgotten dream, I couldn't identify them until I got closer. My heart sank as I studied Lucas.

He looked gaunt, and his once sparkling eyes seemed devoid of color. I wanted to fling my arms around him but instead I stopped a couple of feet away and stood across from him. His clothes hung as though he had borrowed them from someone much larger, and I found myself hoping that was the case, and not that he had lost such a lot of weight.

I opened my mouth to say something, but nothing came out. What was I going to say anyway? *Hey?*

"So, this sucks, huh?" Nate was trying to ease the tension, albeit unsuccessfully; I tried to catch Lucas's eye, and he continued to avoid my gaze.

I kept giving him sideways glances to get a better feel for the changes I couldn't quite pinpoint. He seemed shorter somehow, as if carrying the weight of the world on his shoulders. His face showed the nicks from a dull razor and his eyes the desire to escape.

Finally, I couldn't take the awkward silence anymore. "Hey," I said like an idiot.

He sucked in a deep breath before responding. "Hey." His voice was flat, and he didn't make eye contact with me.

"Can I—" The words choked me, but I made myself go on, "Can I talk to you?" He couldn't mask his surprise and took so long to move that I thought he might say no—but then he nodded and followed me down the hall.

When we were out of earshot of Nate and Mela, who were both looking at us with concern, I stopped and turned to face him.

"I'm so sorry about this. I wish you didn't have to testify."

He shrugged in response. "Don't worry about it."

"I do worry about it. I wish you could get away."

Lucas laughed, but it wasn't the lighthearted chuckle I had

come to know. This laugh was full of bitterness, and I could smell alcohol on his breath.

"It's a subpoena; I can't get away. Let's just get it over with." He ran his hands through his hair and then shoved them into his pocket.

"Lucas," I whispered gently, and his eyes finally connected with mine. They were still my favorite mix of hazel and green, but they lacked the playfulness I remembered. "I'll make sure everyone knows the truth. They'll know it wasn't your fault. You were just protecting me."

"Is that what you've been learning in college? That anyone gives a crap about the truth? Grow up, Liv."

I recoiled. A slap would have been less painful than the words he had just spat at me. For a moment, I thought I saw regret in his eyes, but they darkened so quickly that I couldn't be sure. He turned and sped away as if he couldn't stand to be so close to me for a second longer, and I, too stunned to do anything else, watched him go. Mela stopped him and waved her finger angrily in his face, but I couldn't hear what she was saying. I sank down on the bench beside me and fought hard to keep my composure. There was no way I was walking into that courtroom with a blotchy face from weeping the way I so desperately wanted to.

Don't worry about it, he had said. How could I not? How could I not worry about the boy who'd protected me? The one who'd given me the courage to meet Ali? The one who'd cut Mela's grass when her mom died though we weren't even speaking. *I come from trash. I thought if you knew where I came from…* The words he had spoken outside his mother's trailer returned to me. He had gone to great lengths to keep his past hidden, and now it would be combed through publicly. I couldn't blame him for being angry about that.

Mela plopped down on the bench beside me. "I'm sorry, Liv. He's been like this for a while. What did he say to you?" Her hands were balled into fists like she was ready for a fight.

"It doesn't matter. At least I got to apologize. Come on, it looks like they're starting soon." I stood up and motioned to the crowd of people streaming into the courtroom.

A low hum reverberated around the room as people chatted softly while waiting for the trial to start. Mela and I sat wedged between my parents, and my mom clutched my hand as if we were about to ride a rollercoaster. Mela's dad was beside mine and reached over to give me a squeeze of solidarity. *Stay strong, Liv,* he seemed to be saying. I smiled back at him. On the pew-like bench ahead of us were Nate and his parents, Mr. & Mrs. Martin, and Lucas. A tightness settled in my chest as I realized that none of his family appeared to be there for him.

He fidgeted on the hard bench, and the way his shoulders sagged made me want to wrap my arms around him. I had lost that right, so I simply sat with my hands folded in my lap and looked around the courtroom instead.

The ominous witness box loomed before me, so I averted my gaze and tried to identify the other witnesses. There were a few candidates, but I couldn't be sure. A girl who looked a couple of years younger than me, with red hair and freckles, kept darting her eyes back and forth and flinching at every sound. Her parents, I assumed by the matching red hair and freckles, flanked her, and her dad held his arm around her. *Yeah, I'd be willing to bet she's one of his victims.*

As I looked around the room, I realized how much more easily I could identify people struggling than before working with Soul Care. The signs were subtle, but they were there. Dark circles under the eyes, fingernails bitten to the quick, dull eyes that had lost their sparkle, lips cracked from being chewed… And then there were the movements: jerky and sudden, restless —clothes being smoothed repeatedly, arms being rubbed to self-soothe.

Professor Powell had taught me many of the ways that victims of abuse tried to cope, and I had observed them during the group sessions several times. But it was a whole other thing to be able to pick out strangers in a room full of people and get a pretty good idea of those Chris had affected. I shuddered involuntarily.

By the time the jury came in, I had picked out seven potential witnesses, and my stomach was churning like water circling the drain. Gunner had said there were only five others, and I was hopeful that they had found a couple more. Somehow, none of this seemed real until the twelve jurors walked in and took a seat.

Studying them as closely as I could, I wondered how many of them would be sympathetic to the victims and how many might believe Chris's story. There were six men, and half of them under thirty, while the rest looked between forty and sixty. How many of them might side with Chris? The remaining jurors were women who looked between twenty-five and sixty-five, if I had to wager a guess. Sixty percent were visible minorities ranging from Black to Asian to Indian. The rest were a mix of Caucasian and possibly Hispanic; it was hard to tell.

One of the older female jurors was wearing a patterned skirt that hung below her knees and a matching jacket. Her old-fashioned attire and the way her disapproving gaze swept the courtroom had me questioning whether she would assume we—the victims—had behaved badly or somehow deserved what we had gotten. A younger female juror had blond dreads and a nose ring. She leaned back in her swivel chair with her ankle resting on her knee and seemed to notice the same girls I had. Her eyes stayed trained on each for a moment longer than coincidence would allow, and it made me hope that maybe one of the jurors would be on our side.

The men ranged from impeccably dressed to looking like they had rolled out of bed that morning and remembered they had jury duty. The well-dressed ones were hard to read. One, dressed in black, looked modern; he reminded me of an old teacher I had in tenth grade who was really open-minded and could see through our BS effortlessly. Perhaps he would be able to see through Chris's deception.

Another juror wore something like sweatpants and an old sweater, and didn't give the impression of knowing what the case was about. He kept looking around in confusion, as if waiting for someone to tell him what to do. I scrutinized each, unable to decide who would decide in favor of the victims and who would be fooled by Chris's defense team.

Gunner and Johnson were already at one of the tables in front, looking much more confident than they had the last time I had seen them. As soon as Chris was led into the room, a hushed silence fell over everyone. He was in a fancy-looking suit with cuffs around his wrists, and yet held his head high as if he had nothing to be ashamed of. My pulse raced and my fingernails dug into my palms with rage. I noticed Lucas stiffen in his seat.

The moment Chris sat down his mother let out a sob. It had to be his mother, because she was the only one who looked distraught over his misfortune, and she had the same brown hair and blue eyes as Chris. She was in an expensive dress and wore a pearl necklace. Easier to clutch for dramatic effect, I guessed.

I refused to give her any more attention, and instead glared at Chris's back. His legal team was numerous and moved in unison, almost as though performing some kind of dance. To my surprise, the principal defense lawyer on Chris's team was a woman. I knew he had very little—if any—respect for women, so it seemed like an odd choice to me. She looked young, too; barely thirty. Her skin was tanned like mine, and shoulder-length, thick curly hair framed her face. Her eyes were the color of dark honey. She wore a black suit with a blue blouse and smiled warmly at the rest of her team. Her demeanor was unassuming and even sweet. I was immediately suspicious of her.

As I studied the rest of the lawyers surrounding Chris, a sinking feeling settled in my gut. There was no other possible conclusion: He came from money—and a lot of it. My early suspicion that his family might be rich was confirmed. His dad must be the man comforting his mom, and he was so well put together that he could have come straight from a photo shoot for luxury products. He spoke to the legal team with a scowl and his mouth set in a line of constant disapproval. His arms had been folded across his chest since he'd sat down. He looked at no one but Chris's lawyers, only breaking away at one point to glance over at Gunner, staring him up and down as though sizing him up for a fight. I hated him immediately and heard Mela huff beside me; no doubt she had come to the same conclusion.

Someone whispered profuse apologies as she squeezed her way through the people on our bench to sit beside my mom. I was surprised to see that it was my sister Amanda. She reached over and squeezed my hand, and there was no trace of I-told-you-so on her face at all. If anything, she looked guilty—as if she should have done more to stop me from seeing Chris. I squeezed her hand back and tried to convey how much it meant to me that she was there, and that I didn't hold her responsible for anything. We smiled at each other quickly and turned to face the front as the bailiff called us all to stand.

Here we go.

17

"*All rise. This court is now in session with the Honorable Judge Harper presiding.*"

After the bailiff finished speaking, he took his position off to the side. The judge was a heavyset black woman with long braided hair and half-moon spectacles. Her face and no-nonsense vibe reminded me of Ruby. She paid little attention to the rest of the courtroom and instead focused her attention on the two legal teams before her. I had no way of knowing, but my first impression was that she'd be a fair judge. Her gavel came down and I bit the inside of my cheek to prevent myself from giving in to the urge to vomit over everyone in my immediate vicinity.

"Stop bouncing," Mela whispered; her tone told me I'd been doing it for a while.

"Sorry," I whispered back.

The opening statements started with Gunner.

"This trial is about power. Throughout this case you will learn that Chris Jamieson was several years older than each of his victims when he took advantage of them. The prosecution will show that this is a man who from his early twenties targeted teenage girls flattered by his attentions, introverts with a degree of alienation from their families, girls who would prefer to suffer in silence rather than confess to adults they had been the victims of sexual abuse. Each of his victims said no. Each of them told him to stop. We will show that he believed that his family's wealth and privilege put him above the law even when assaulting minors.

"Ladies and gentlemen of the jury, for the duration of this trial the state will present evidence that proves beyond a reasonable doubt that the defendant used his power and privilege to physically overcome his victims' resistance to his unwanted sexual advances. The evidence will prove that over a period of three years, Chris Jamieson preyed on young girls, forced himself on them in various ways, and that he is guilty of all the crimes he has been charged with. After you have heard that evidence, the state will ask that you find him guilty as charged."

Other than the part about my being an alienated introvert, the statement made me want to stand up and start a slow clap, but I was pretty sure that would get me kicked out of the room. The judge appeared unmoved by Gunner's statement, but I could see that some of the younger jury members were disturbed by the allegations. *Good.*

Chris's primary lawyer, Defense Attorney McElroy, stood and spoke directly to the jury. "Chris Jamieson is a twenty-four-year-old senior manager at a prestigious finance company. He has lived in the Fort Lauderdale area all his life and was the valedictorian of his graduating class. He has always been popular and well liked, whether at school, work, or socially, and has never had any trouble with the law—not even a parking ticket.

"Throughout this trial, you will hear evidence that Chris met and courted several young women over a period of three years. He took these women out, paid for their expenses, bought them gifts, and treated them very well. We will prove that the young women who claim to have been attacked were with him of their own free will, and in fact saw him or contacted him again after they broke up. That many never came forward, probably not thinking that anything untoward had happened. We will prove that this is simply a case of another young man being dragged before the law in the wake of 'metoo' just for courting a girl. You will need to decide whether or not you believe beyond a reasonable doubt that the charges against him are in fact warranted.

"I submit that after you hear all the evidence presented and have the opportunity to judge the credibility of the witnesses, the state will not prove to you beyond a reasonable doubt that Mr. Jamieson is guilty as charged. I will then come back to you and ask that you find Chris Jamieson not guilty."

Mela and I exchanged wary glances. McElroy might have looked sweet, but I had a feeling she was anything but.

Before long, Johnson was calling the DA's first witness.

"The prosecution calls Madison Hillcrest to the witness stand."

I was surprised to see that it was the redhead I had picked out before. Gunner had told me the first witness was meant to create the biggest effect on the jury. I watched her practically tiptoe to get sworn in at the stand, and I hoped the dark feeling covering me like a shadow was wrong. Her face was so pale that her freckles seemed to jump out as though they were three dimensional. She wore an olive-green dress that hung below her knees and a small white sweater partly buttoned. The way she gripped her crucifix necklace almost made me want to pray right alongside her.

"Miss Hillcrest, can you tell us how old you are?" Johnson began.

"I—I'm eighteen. I just turned eighteen." Madison's voice squeaked like a mouse's.

"And when did you meet the defendant, Mr. Jamieson?"

"Umm, about six months ago, I think."

"Did he pursue you romantically?"

"Mmmhmm. Yes, yes, he did."

Johnson had been about to say something, and I guessed it was along the lines of needing a more definitive answer than mmmhmm. Madison must have picked up on that. I shifted in my seat as I watched one of the old-fashioned jurors raise her eyebrows.

After a few minutes of back and forth between them to establish that Chris was older and Madison a minor at the time of the alleged assault, Johnson started getting into the tougher questions.

"Could you tell us what happened the night of the attack?"

"We had gone to see a movie, but instead of driving me home after, he drove me to a place I'd never been before and pulled over on the side of the road." Her shaking hands were visible to everyone in the courtroom.

"Were there lots of vehicles driving by or was it secluded?" Johnson probed.

"There was no one else around. It was dark. There weren't even any streetlights on that road."

Johnson nodded. "What happened next?"

"Well, he, uhh—" She looked over at her parents as though willing them to leave, and her face flushed a shade of crimson that made me embarrassed for her as she continued. "He started kissing me and pulled my hand onto his…lap." Shifting awkwardly in her seat, she looked down, likely to hide her blush from the public, but the tips of her ears gave her away.

"And what did you do in response?" Johnson tried to be delicate, but the subject matter made it difficult.

"I pulled my hand away and told him that I was late for curfew, and I needed to go home."

"And what did he say?"

"He said that I needed to stop acting like a child, and that if I didn't do what he wanted, he would leave me on the side of the road by myself. I had left my phone at home because we were going to a movie, so I wouldn't have been able to call anyone for help." Her voice seemed to be pleading with us to understand.

"Did you do what he wanted you to do?"

"Yes." Her voice was a whisper.

"And what exactly—"

I didn't want to know what exactly he had made her do. Bouncing my right knee to the tune of the song I was humming in my head helped to distract me from what was being discussed.

"Afterwards he said, 'I've had worse' and then he drove me home and never called me again." Madison's eyes were red and puffy as she wiped her nose with the tissue someone had provided her.

"Did you tell your parents what happened?"

"No; no, I couldn't." Her face flushed with a new round of shame.

"Why not?" Johnson asked.

She looked at Johnson helplessly. "My parents had warned me repeatedly about not being alone with boys. I thought they'd be furious if I told them what had happened."

"No further questions, Your Honor."

Johnson returned to her desk as Chris's defense team huddled together before McElroy broke off from the group and began her line of questioning.

"To be clear, you and Mr. Jamieson have never slept together, correct?"

"Right." Madison's tone was clipped.

"And the night in question, Mr. Jamieson didn't physically overpower you or force you to perform any sexual acts, correct?"

"Well, no. I guess he didn't physically force me. But—"

"Just a yes or no will do, thank you. You mentioned that Mr. Jamieson never called you again. Were you hoping he would?" McElroy cocked her head to the side as though genuinely curious.

"No, of course not," Madison stammered.

"It seems like an odd thing to say if this experience was as awful as you claim. You could have gotten out of the car at any time, isn't that right?"

"I...it was raining." She looked around helplessly.

"So, staying in the car with Mr. Jamieson was a better option to you than standing outside in the rain?"

"I didn't know where I was or anything." Her voice now quivered. "It was so dark and secluded…"

"Isn't it more likely that you never told any adults because you wished to begin your sexual life freely and in secret, as most teenagers do, and were deeply attracted to the defendant?"

"No, that's not true—"

Madison burst into tears, and it took several minutes for her to calm down enough to continue answering questions. I watched the jury carefully and didn't like what I saw. The jurors who looked older than forty seemed thoroughly unmoved. The oldest female juror was pursing her lips and shaking her head slightly, but in judgment of Madison instead of Chris. They looked unconvinced that the experience had been as horrible as the girl claimed.

"So, you chose to stay in the car knowing what would happen, right?" McElroy was really driving her point home.

"W-what could I do…" Madison hiccupped.

"Yes or no?"

"Yes, but—"

"No further questions, Your Honor." McElroy threw what I considered to be a smug smile in Chris's direction and sat beside him.

Dread was filling me as quickly as a boulder that had been pushed off a cliff. Soon enough it would be my turn, and I wasn't sure I'd fare any better than she had.

18

It was here. The moment I had been dreading since I'd found out it would happen.

"The defense calls Lucas O'Connell to the witness stand."

It hurt to hear his name called. I couldn't help myself; I reached over and squeezed his shoulder, and my heart skipped a beat when he leaned back into it for just a second as though he were drawing strength. He stood up slowly and walked to the front of the room to get sworn in. When he turned and sat in the witness box, I nearly gasped. I had never seen him so pale. Mela squeezed my hand as another of Chris's defense attorney's, Wright I think his name was, stood up to begin the questioning.

He wasted no time.

"Mr. O'Connell, how did you come to meet my client?" His lips were turned up with a smug I-know-something-you-don't look on his face. It made me shudder.

Lucas cleared his throat before leaning toward the microphone and responding. "My girlfriend told me that he was stalking her, and I found him watching her from the parking lot of her work."

"You found him in his car in that parking lot, you mean. He

wasn't physically near her, correct?" The defense had hardly let him finish his sentence.

"Well, n-no, I guess not," he stammered.

The defense smiled and continued.

"Isn't it true that the first time you met my client, you physically assaulted him to the degree that he was hospitalized, and you were then arrested for it?"

Lucas swallowed hard and nodded. "Yes." He was looking down as he answered.

"And isn't it true that this wasn't your first brush with violence? Didn't you also get expelled from your first high school for fighting?"

My eyes darted to Nate's, and the wince on his face told me it was true. I hadn't ever asked Lucas about why he'd wound up at Banting.

"How did you...?" Lucas looked confused.

Wright walked back to the defense desk, where Chris sat, and took a piece of paper from a folder. "Your Honor, I'd like to show the defendant's exhibit A to the witness."

"All right," the judge answered.

Gunner and Johnson searched through their copy of exhibits registered as Wright walked to the witness stand and put it down in front of Lucas.

"Would you please tell the court what it is I've just handed you?"

Lucas looked at it warily. "It says defendant's exhibit A, official letter of expulsion for Lucas O'Connell."

"Would you now read line five?"

Lucas sighed and read. "Reason for expulsion: physically assaulting another male student." He ran his hands through his hair.

"Is this a fair and accurate copy of the exhibit?"

"Yes."

"Mr. O'Connell, you have a pattern of physically assaulting people, don't you?"

"Objection. Leading." Johnson had stood up to address the judge.

"I'll rephrase." Wright looked completely unfazed. "Isn't it possible that my client being in the parking lot that night had nothing to do with your girlfriend?"

"No, it isn't. He was clearly there for her." I saw the knuckles on Lucas's hands whiten with the force he was using to control his anger.

Wright narrowed his eyes slightly but didn't press him on it.

"You grew up on welfare, correct?" The smug look on the lawyer's face had returned.

"How is that relevant?" Lucas demanded.

"Please answer the question, Mr. O'Connell." It was the judge this time.

"Yes, my mom was on government assistance." He spoke the words through clenched teeth.

"And struggling, I'd imagine, based on the numerous eviction notices she's had for non-payment." Wright referred to a stack of papers as defendant exhibits B through H.

I swallowed the bile at the back of my throat, imagining how often he'd had to move as a kid.

"And your father?" Wright angled his head to the side as though he didn't know the answer.

"What about my father?" Lucas's cheeks were getting pinker by the minute.

"What age were you when he skipped town?"

"Objection. Relevance." This time it was Gunner.

"I am establishing Mr. O'Connell's character as it pertains to this case." The defense lawyer's eyes widened as he pretended to be confused by Gunner's objection.

"I'll allow it, but get to your point, Counselor." The judge looked at Lucas for his answer.

"Three. I was three when he left."

My heart ached as he struggled on the stand.

"Did your mother remarry?"

"No."

"Any long-time boyfriends?"

"Not really, no."

The defense lawyer pursed his lips and stroked his chin thoughtfully. "Were you living with your mom when you sent my client to the hospital?"

"No."

"Where were you living?"

"I was staying with a friend and his parents."

"So you were essentially homeless."

Mrs. Martin's back stiffened and she whispered something angrily to her husband. This wasn't going well.

"I guess you could say that." Lucas looked resigned; he was losing any fight he had come with.

"And now you live with your older brother, is that right?"

"Yes."

"He's been in and out of jail several times has he not?"

"Objection. Relevance." Gunner sounded pissed. *Good.*

The defense lawyer smiled. "I'll withdraw. So, at the time of meeting Mr. Jamieson, you were fatherless, homeless, had a history of violence, no real stability in terms of housing throughout your childhood, attending an alternate high school after getting expelled, and then arrested for his assault. Is that about right?"

"Yeah, but—"

The defense interjected. "We just need a yes or no."

"Yes." Lucas's eyes flashed angrily.

"No further questions, Your Honor."

Gunner stood up quickly and approached the witness stand.

"Mr. O'Connell, how did you meet Olivia Jackson?"

"I was running on the beach one day and accidentally ran into her. She fell and I helped her up." His eyes darted to mine for a quick second, and I smiled at the memory.

"How did she seem?"

"Objection. Relevance," McElroy said.

"Your Honor, I'm establishing how Ms. Jackson appeared shortly after her altercation with Mr. Jamieson."

"I'll allow it," the judge said, and nodded to Lucas to continue.

"She looked scared, like I was about to attack her. Her fists were clenched, and her eyes were all over the place. But then she relaxed when I helped her up."

I grimaced, imagining how I must have looked that day. We never talked about it, and I hadn't realized that he had noticed how jumpy I was.

"Mr. O'Connell, what was Chris Jamieson doing when you found him in the parking lot on the night in question?"

"He had just been inside Olivia's place of work, and I could see how rattled she was. He returned to his car and continued to stare at her while she tried to work." His jaw flexed as he seemed to remember how Chris looked that night.

"He wasn't distracted by anything? Wasn't playing on his phone?"

Lucas shook his head immediately. "No, his eyes were locked on her and moved to wherever she was in Brew."

"What happened next?"

"I stormed over to his car and yanked him out; told him to stop preying on her."

"And what was his response to that?" Wright asked.

"Olivia had come outside, and he laughed while asking her if I was his replacement. I told him not to talk to her."

"How did he react?"

"He laughed even harder, and Olivia told him to leave. He said he'd leave if she left her trailer-trash boyfriend and got back together with him."

"And what did you do then?"

"I punched him in the face." Lucas glanced nervously at the judge.

"What was going through your mind during that fight?"

"I just wanted to protect Olivia. Chris was never going to

leave her alone; I could see that. I thought if he knew he'd have a fight coming the next time he tried to see her, it might deter him from continuing to scare her."

"So, you were just trying to protect your girlfriend, who was afraid of her ex. Is that right?"

"That's right," Lucas said.

"No further questions, Your Honor."

Much to my dismay, Wright stood up to cross examine Lucas. I had been hoping he'd be able to get off the stand.

"Mr. O'Connell, isn't it possible that my client, coming from a stable home, working full time, renting his own place, and owning his own vehicle triggered you into violence that night?"

"I didn't know anything about him other than how scared Olivia was of him," Lucas snapped, making me wince in my seat.

"And that was enough justification in your mind to send a man to the hospital." It wasn't a question. Wright looked over at the jury as though daring them to come to any conclusion other than the picture he had just effortlessly painted of a criminal in the making.

I could feel my mom side-eying me, so I stared straight ahead. Lucas wasn't the violent psychopath Wright was making him out to be. If my mom had known him like I did, she wouldn't be staring at me.

"If Miss Jackson was as distraught as you say when you met her, I wonder: Why would you have gotten into a relationship with someone like that?"

"With someone like what?"

"Someone whose mental state was so fragile."

"Olivia isn't *fragile,*" he responded angrily.

"Well, which is it Mr. O'Connell? Either she is a strong woman able to handle herself, or she's fragile and needed someone to take care of her."

"I—" Lucas tried to speak but was cut off before he could say anything.

"Wouldn't you agree that what actually set you off that night was Mr. Jamieson calling you trailer trash? It's no secret that you grew up in difficult circumstances and that your mother resides in a trailer. Could it be that you were trying to shut Chris up before he exposed you?"

"I was just trying to protect my girlfriend," he muttered.

"So, she knew how you grew up then? No secrets between you?"

"Objection. Relevance."

"Your Honor, I'm merely suggesting an alternative motive than the one that's been presented."

The judge seemed to ponder Wright's argument for a moment. "Answer the question, Mr. O'Connell."

"No, she didn't know how I grew up." Lucas looked defeated. This was exactly what I had feared, and it was coming true before my eyes.

"No further questions, Your Honor."

Wright turned and walked over to his desk to sit beside Chris, who was the picture of solemn calm. I glared at the back of his neck, willing it to spontaneously combust. At that moment, I envied Lucas for having punched him in the face several times.

My eyes darted to and from the jury, but it was hard to tell which way they were leaning. Rage burned in the pit of my stomach. They had no right to judge Lucas. *Except that's literally their job right now, Liv.*

As soon as the session ended, Lucas shot out of the courtroom. I tried to catch his eye, but he wouldn't look at me. The expression on his face destroyed me. I knew he already believed that he came from trash, and now Chris's defense team had proved that to everyone. I vowed right then and there that they would not break me, and that I would find a way to make things right with Lucas before this was all over. It was my turn on the stand next, and I was just mad enough to do a good job.

19

"Ms. Jackson, can you tell the court what happened that night in September, two years ago?" Gunner was asking the questions today.

I took a deep breath before responding. "Chris and I had gone out for dinner to celebrate our three-month anniversary. Afterwards, he drove me to his apartment." A tremor began to run through my hands.

"Did you know you'd be at his apartment alone?" Gunner knew my story well, so I understood that these questions were strategic.

"No. I thought he was driving me home until I realized that I didn't recognize where we were."

"You were nervous about going, weren't you?"

"Objection. Leading." Wright was on it.

"Sustained. Please rephrase your question, Counselor." The judge gave Gunner a you-know-better look.

"How were you feeling about going to his apartment?" Gunner was unfazed by what had just happened, so I followed his lead.

"I was uneasy. Honestly, I didn't know where we were going until he pulled up to an apartment building. He told me he had a surprise for me." Resisting the urge to shake my head at my own idiocy for ever being with him, I pressed my tongue against the inside of my teeth until it hurt.

"How old were you both at that time?"

"I was sixteen and he was twenty-two." A murmur went through the courtroom at that little tidbit. The look on my dad's face was murderous.

"Okay, so you got to his apartment building, and then what happened?"

"I wanted to go home, but I didn't think he'd understand, so eventually I got out of the car and followed him up."

"Why didn't you think he'd understand that you wanted to go home?" Gunner sounded genuinely confused, but we had role played this, so I knew he wasn't.

"Chris was always telling me how mature I was. I guess I didn't want to disappoint him."

"What happened when you got up to his apartment?"

"He gave me a tour and asked if I wanted to go into his bedroom with him. I said no. We went into the living room, and I sat in the chair instead of on the couch beside him." I remembered arguing how irrelevant all these details were when we role played, but Johnson had assured me that they mattered, so I didn't leave anything out.

"Was he happy about your seating choice?" Gunner asked.

"No. He was offended that I was sitting far away, so I made myself sit with him on his couch."

"Did you want to be there?" Gunner asked bluntly.

"No."

"Then why didn't you leave?"

"I thought I was just being childish. We hadn't even had a conversation about taking things to the next level, so I didn't think that…" I trailed off. *That he would try to rape me.* "I thought I could trust him."

"So, you were sitting beside him on the couch. What happened next?"

This was where I hadn't wanted to go. Hesitating, I searched for Lucas. He was still sullen, and when our eyes met, he looked startled. A moment passed between us, and his face began to change. Almost as if his chivalry was coming through despite his rough exterior, he nodded me on, and I could feel his support. Drawing strength from him, I continued.

"Chris put his arm around me and pulled me closer. When I resisted, he told me to relax. He kissed me, and when I tried to pull away, he got annoyed. He kissed me harder and pushed me down on the couch so that he was on top of me. I told him no, but he kept going."

Clearing my throat, I stared hard at the gleaming polished wood on the witness stand to avoid seeing the look on my friends' and family's faces.

"I tried to push him off me, but I wasn't strong enough. I screamed, but I was muffled by his hand over my mouth. He unbuttoned my jeans, and that was when I knew he wasn't going to stop." My voice broke.

"Take your time." Gunner sounded sympathetic even while looking increasingly uncomfortable.

No one made a sound as I collected myself and went on. "He told me I didn't need to be scared, and that it was going to feel amazing—that I would love it. I was sobbing and he was undoing his pants and forcing my knees up." Swallowing hard as I remembered exactly how I felt when it was happening, I made myself continue. "'I've been dying to be your first.' That's what he said as he forced himself on me. The only reason he didn't succeed was because his roommate came into the room unexpectedly and confronted him. I ran out of his apartment without even putting my shoes on." The tremor in my hands had grown steadily and they were now shaking even as I tried to hold them still.

"Did he pursue you?"

I nodded. "Yes, he came after me and tried to make me get into his car."

"What happened next?"

"I called my best friend and her and her boyfriend came to find me and drove me back to her place."

"Why didn't you go home?" Gunner jutted his chin questioningly.

"I didn't want my parents to see how upset I was. They would have known something was wrong."

"Would that have been a bad thing?"

I bit my lip before answering. "Yes, it would have. My dad really didn't like Chris to begin with, and they had always told me to be careful when it came to guys. I didn't want to let them down, so I tried to deal with it myself." I avoided looking over at my parents, not wanting them to think I hadn't trusted them. It was much more complicated than that.

Gunner asked me many more questions about that night and the night Chris was hospitalized. It felt like I was on the stand for hours, and I knew that Chris's team was going to drag me through the mud with their line of questioning. The only person I looked at was Gunner because I couldn't bear to see how anyone else was responding to me retelling the events of the worst night of my life. I didn't want their pity, but I also didn't want to see that they didn't believe me. Long before I was ready, McElroy was probing into my life.

"Where did you celebrate your three-month anniversary with my client, Miss Jackson?"

"Bernard's." I had been giving her one-word answers for a few minutes. Johnson had told me never to offer more than I was asked, and I intended to follow that advice.

"What kind of restaurant was it?"

"One that serves food." My voice went up at the end like I was asking a question. A few chuckles echoed around the room.

"What I mean is, was it a fancy restaurant? Expensive?"

"Yes."

"Did you pay for your meal or did Mr. Jamieson?" McElroy's look of understanding made it seem she could relate to my story.

I forced myself to remember that she wasn't on my side, no matter how sweet she looked.

"Chris paid."

"Did he pay for your dates often?"

I didn't like where she was going with these questions. *What, because he paid for my food, I was obligated to sleep with him?* "Yes."

"Is it fair to say that you knew he had substantial means?"

"No, I didn't."

McElroy submitted receipts as evidence for every date I'd ever gone on with Chris, including gas receipts for the times he drove me anywhere. They totaled over $1,500. I couldn't believe he'd kept a tally.

"Let's talk about the night in question. You celebrated your anniversary with my client. He paid for an expensive dinner and then took you back to his apartment. You went up with him willingly, yes?"

"Like I said, I didn't want to go up."

"But you did go, and you weren't physically forced to, correct?"

"Correct." The anger within me was gaining traction.

"And then, as per your own testimony, you sat beside him on his couch and let him kiss you. What did you think was going to happen?" Her tone made me feel like a silly child who had eaten too much candy and gotten a stomachache.

"I hadn't had time to think about what was going to happen. I didn't even know we were going to his apartment until we were already there."

"Why didn't you tell him to stop?" She looked genuinely baffled.

"I said no." The words came through my clenched teeth.

"But did you actually say *stop*?"

I racked my brain and reluctantly gave her the answer I knew she was expecting. "I guess not."

"So couldn't he have just thought you were being shy—bashful, even?"

"I was crying and thrashing to get away. No means no."

"So *you* say. What were you wearing that night?" She pressed a pen to her lips as though she were truly trying to comprehend every angle of the scenario.

"Jeans and a tank top." My voice was flat.

"Was the tank top form-fitting?"

I sighed. "Yes." Knowing where she was going with this didn't make it any less disgusting.

"So you let my client pay for your expensive dinner, went up to his apartment wearing little more than lingerie— my mouth fell open in protest but she continued— "sat with him on the couch, let him kiss you, and you want us to believe that you didn't want to sleep with him?" She looked over at the jury as though saying, *Come on, you know she's lying.*

I clenched my shaking hands into fists and calmed myself with the mental image of me punching McElroy in the face the way I had with Katie. *Think of your happy place, Liv; don't give her what she wants.* There was no happy place, though. I searched the courtroom and my eyes fell on Madison, who still looked terrified. I remembered how she had fallen apart on the stand and suddenly I was saying something on her behalf, for which I knew I'd get in trouble.

"Why don't you ask your client why the girls he likes have to be underage and vulnerable? Why doesn't he have relationships with women his own age?"

"Objection! Move to strike from the record," McElroy cried.

Johnson and Gunner were both staring at me as I nervously tapped my foot against the floor.

"Sustained." Judge Harper turned to the jury and continued. "The last two questions are stricken from the record. Members of the jury, you must disregard them."

Then, to my horror, Judge Harper turned to Gunner and Johnson. "Counselors, please contain your witness."

They nodded solemnly. I had been admonished without even

being spoken to, and my words had simply been erased from the record.

Before I could collect myself, McElroy was already asking me another question.

"Did you know Mr. O'Connell while you were dating my client?"

My eyes flashed to Lucas's before answering. "No."

"But he was living with your best friend's boyfriend at the time was he not?"

"Yes, I believe so."

"Do you expect the court to believe that you didn't already know him?"

"Objection. Relevance." Johnson looked annoyed.

"I have a point, Your Honor."

"Then get to it, Counselor. Overruled. Please answer the question, Miss Jackson." I wasn't sure how well this was going. It seemed she was trying to convince the jury that I was a liar.

"It's the truth. We only met six weeks after…that night."

"So just a few weeks later, you were already in another relationship?"

"It was longer than that."

"How much longer? Seven weeks? Eight?"

"I don't recall." Gunner had advised me to use that when I couldn't remember the exact details.

"Why did you come forward now?" She caught me off guard with her new line of questioning.

"Excuse me?" I stammered.

"Why now? Why not the night in question? Or the night your boyfriend was arrested? Why would you wait more than two years to come forward?"

"At the time I was afraid that Chris would press charges against Lucas. I didn't want his future to be affected." Out of the corner of my eye I saw my mom turn and say something to my dad. I was glad I couldn't hear them.

"And how exactly did you get Mr. Jamieson to agree not to

press charges? I'd imagine he would have been rather inclined to keep Mr. O'Connell locked up."

"I threatened to release a recording of Chris admitting to trying to rape me." My voice sounded hollow in my ears. The recording had been deemed inadmissible in court.

"So, you blackmailed my client." It wasn't a question.

I couldn't help but scoff. *Blackmailed? Please.* "I wouldn't call it that."

"Well, you made him agree to something he didn't want to do while holding something over his head. That's blackmail."

I bit the inside of my lip to stop myself from saying something I'd regret.

"Do you want to know what I think?" McElroy went on without waiting for an answer from me, which was probably best because it would have been no, I didn't want to know what she thought. "I think that you and Mr. O'Connell knew that my client was well off, and you thought you'd take advantage of that. Your best friend's boyfriend was harboring him at the time, and I'm sure you don't expect the jury to believe you didn't already know him. I think it was always your plan to blackmail Mr. Jamieson, but you had to alter those plans after Mr. O'Connell got arrested."

Fury built up inside me like water in a dam about to burst, yet instead of letting the rage out, I became calm. Maybe the calmest I had ever been in my entire life.

McElroy's demeaning and fictional summary was maddening, but I couldn't let myself get angry. Johnson had told me to speak from the heart.

"I was sixteen, and Chris Jamieson was older. His attention was flattering, and my self-esteem was in the gutter at the time. I didn't know he came from money; that wouldn't have mattered to me. All I knew was that he was an older guy who really seemed to like me, and that was nice. Lucas and I didn't meet until weeks after Chris and I had broken up because I was too scared to leave my house. I wouldn't even go to my best friend's place. I never expected things to go so badly."

My shoulders slumped under the weight of all my confessions. I braced myself as I waited for her rebuttal. Every question she asked was challenged by Gunner and Johnson before I could answer. It was like watching a tennis match between them, only I was the ball.

The judge eventually had both sides approach the bench, where a flurry of whispered conversations ensued. I sat glued to my seat, frustrated that I couldn't just get up and leave. The witness box was beginning to close in on me. How much longer would I have to sit up there like a thing on display? Was it getting hotter? The lights seemed brighter than they had a few minutes before. A bead of sweat trickled down my back as I forced myself to remain perfectly still. I wouldn't give Chris or his defense team the satisfaction of knowing they were getting to me.

"You may step down, Miss Jackson." The judge's voice broke my concentration.

My head jerked up; I wanted to see whether I had just imagined her dismissing me. She gestured for me to leave the box, so I stood up quickly and made myself put one shaking leg in front of the other until I was back in my seat. Why hadn't McElroy drilled me with more questions? I was sure I had missed something important while I daydreamed about being literally anywhere else. Mela squeezed my hand and made a face at how sweaty it was. I nearly laughed out loud but caught myself just in time. The relief flooding through me was intoxicating. I had done it. Hopefully I had convinced the jury that Chris was a monster, but only time would tell.

The real question was whether it was going to be enough.

20

My parents looked like they wanted to say a lot to me but unfortunately for them, my sole focus was on making Lucas talk to me as soon as court was adjourned for the day.

The sound of the gavel coming down might as well have been the starting gun at the beginning of a race, the way he shot out of his seat and rounded the corner before I could even stand up. Someone grabbed my wrist, but I shook it off as I squeezed past Mela and practically ran down the courtroom aisle. Once I was in the hall and past several reporters waiting by the doors, my eyes darted back and forth, scanning the room for Lucas. He was nowhere to be found.

"Damn," I mumbled as Mela came up behind me.

"Where's the fire?" She was out of breath, having chased after me.

"I was trying to catch Lucas before he left, but I hadn't anticipated him having trained for the Olympics." My lips pursed together in frustration as Mela's eyes widened at something she was seeing behind me.

Whipping around, I saw my parents approaching; by their faces, I understood why Mela was now retreating almost as quickly as Lucas had. I tried to grab her hand to make her stay with me, but she dodged it expertly and threw me a good-luck-with-everything look as she hopped onto the elevator and disappeared.

"I'm going to tear his arms off and beat him to death with them." My dad was angrier than I had ever seen him before.

"Shh, Dad. What if someone hears you and then that happens? You'll be the prime suspect." My efforts to lighten the mood failed miserably.

"Why didn't you come to us? I thought we were closer than that, Liv." The agony on his face pierced my heart but seeing him like this was exactly why I hadn't gone to them.

My mom had an apprehensive look, which I knew meant she had something to say and wasn't sure how to say it.

I sighed. "Just say it, Mom."

"I'm really sorry for what you went through, Olivia. It's unimaginable. But now that I know all the gory details, how could you not have turned Chris in to the police?" She sounded dumbfounded.

"Like I said on the stand—"

She cut me off and interjected. "For *Lucas*?" She spat his name like it was a bad taste in her mouth.

"Yes, for *Lucas*," I hissed back.

"So, you let the rest of the girls in that courtroom be traumatized by that monster to protect a *boy*? Some of them went through the same thing you did—or worse—*after* you, and you could have stopped it if you had just turned him in." Her eyes were wide with disbelief.

I shook my head and backed away from her. She had stabbed me right in the heart of my insecurities. Of course I felt guilty about that, but had I really been prepared to see Lucas thrown in jail?

"Olivia?" Gunner was standing off to the side awkwardly; he had heard the conversation between us and felt obligated to step in.

I cleared my throat before speaking. "Yeah?"

He looked from me to my parents as Johnson came up behind him to join the conversation.

"Olivia, great job in there," Johnson said without seeming to notice she had just interrupted a very awkward standoff. She shook her head as she answered my unspoken question. "It was a strong testimony, and it might have been enough, only…" She trailed off.

I held my breath while I waited for one of them to give me the bad news. They exchanged a glance and Gunner spoke.

"Most of the other witnesses have pulled out of testifying. We only have one left, and her testimony is pretty weak." His tone was matter-of-fact, but the look on his face was pained. He wanted Chris behind bars maybe as much as I did.

"Why would they do that?" My words came out with difficulty, and I forced myself to release my jaw.

"It was Madison's testimony. They got scared seeing her lose it on the stand like that. They don't think they can be as strong as you were in the face of McElroy's badgering. Not to mention how badly they picked on Lucas." Johnson's tone was sympathetic.

"So, what does this mean?" The question came from my mom. I had forgotten that she and my dad were still standing there.

"It means," Gunner responded in a clipped tone, "that if we can't convince those girls to testify, Chris will most likely go free."

I sucked in my breath as my parents argued with them. Dropping to the bench beside me, I put my head in my hands and let my hair cover my face. If only I could block out all the noise. How could it have come to this? I had thought the hard part was over. That I had risen to the occasion and told the truth, and that was to be the end of it. *So much for the truth setting you free.*

"Maybe I can talk to them," I mumbled through my hair.

"Talk to who? The other victims? Olivia, please." My Mom sounded exasperated.

Risking a glance at her, I regretted it immediately. I hadn't thought it was such a stupid idea, but now I wasn't so sure.

"She's right, you can't talk to them. Chris's defense team could accuse you of conspiring with them and get the case thrown out on a technicality," Johnson said.

I clicked my shoes together. *There's no place like home, there's no place like home.* Only "home" at the moment was Mela's, and I found myself missing the safety of my dorm room back in New York. At least it was hundreds of miles from Florida.

Johnson, Gunner, and my mom kept talking as I felt my dad plop down beside me and put his arm around my shoulders. A lifetime of sitting beside him made the familiarity of his gesture comforting. I breathed in his aftershave, and it made me want to crawl onto his lap.

"Your mother's love language is fear, Liv. She's not angry with you, she's scared—more scared than I've ever seen her," he murmured gently in my ear.

My eyes prickled with unshed tears. Even though I understood what he meant, it still stung to have her respond to me like that. It was enough to make me want to go back to New York and leave Florida behind. But I knew that was just the pain talking. There was no time for a pity party, no matter how much I deserved one.

My dad squeezed my shoulder one more time and stood up to join the dwindling conversation. After a few more minutes, Gunner and Johnson excused themselves to go talk strategy. They let me know they'd be in touch if anything changed, but neither of them looked particularly hopeful.

Reluctantly I stood up. My shoulders felt as though someone had filled them with concrete, and I could hardly find the strength to straighten them. Suddenly my mom pulled me into her arms and squeezed me so tightly I could hardly breathe.

"I love you." She whispered the words in my ear, and before I could respond she had released me and was retreating quickly to the elevators.

My dad shrugged again and gave me a look that seemed to say, *Your guess is as good as mine* before he followed her. I stayed back, opting to take the next elevator—having reached my limit of awkward conversations for the day.

Once back in the safety of Mela's car, I filled her in on what had happened.

"So, it was all for nothing?" she cried, matching my emotions like only a best friend could.

"Looks like it." What else could I do? I had given it my all on the witness stand. There was nothing to be done. And yet I had the sneaking suspicion that I wouldn't rest until I had thought of something.

It can't end like this, can it?

21

The smell of coffee filled the air, and I sniffed appreciatively as I shuffled toward the counter at Brew, still half asleep. I felt like a zombie, having tossed and turned the night before. Grateful for the weekend and no court for two days, I had rolled out of bed just after six in the morning, abandoning any hope of getting solid sleep. Instead, I opted to walk over to my old workplace and enjoy the familiarity of a latte surrounded by books and old coworkers.

I was greeted warmly by Jenna, who had taken my role as supervisor when I left for school. She insisted my latte was on the house, and I resisted the urge to throw my arms around her. *Feeling a little nostalgic, are we?* Inwardly laughing at myself, I chose a booth by one of the bookcases. I sipped my drink and looked through the books absentmindedly before finally choosing one to sit down with.

Before I knew it, two hours had gone by, and I was still fully engrossed in the book. Jenna brought me another latte and a breakfast sandwich, which I devoured almost before she had put the plate down. The book I'd chosen was written by a twenty-something woman who had been sexually assaulted while she was unconscious, and what she endured afterwards through a very public trial. I couldn't put it down.

"That's quite a book, huh?" Jenna's blue eyes pierced me curiously.

"Have you read it?"

"I started to, but it was pretty intense. That girl has been through a lot."

"Yeah, she has," I murmured thoughtfully. "It's too bad other women didn't come forward because, you know, he more than likely assaulted more than just her."

"Oh, absolutely. Guys like that always do."

An idea was brewing in my mind as I remembered the reporters outside the courtroom. What I needed was a story more powerful than mine that had nothing to do with Chris. I slid out of the booth so quickly I nearly knocked Jenna down.

"Sorry, I just remembered I'm supposed to be somewhere. Thank you for this morning, it was just what I needed." After squeezing her arm affectionately, I hurried out the door and scanned the parking lot for the vehicle I forgot hadn't driven there. *Crap. Looks like I'm walking.*

The library was a good twenty-minute walk away, but fueled by lattes Jenna had most likely spiked with a shot of espresso, I was practically flying down the paths that led there. In less than fifteen minutes, I was standing before a tall building with white pillars framing the doorway. I had timed it perfectly since it had just opened and only a couple of librarians could be seen walking around.

"Excuse me…" I stopped the one closest to me, but I was still out of breath, and she started in surprise.

"Yes?" She didn't look older than thirty, and wore dress slacks and a colorful top. The hair framing her face was dyed blue. Librarians had really come a long way from hair in tight buns, knitted cardigans and glasses attached by a thin chain sliding down their noses. Clearly, I had been watching too many old movies lately.

"I'm wondering if you can direct me to search for local sexual assault cases over the last ten to fifteen years." Even as I said it, I knew that I could have searched for this information online at Mela's, but I wasn't ready to talk about this plan yet.

"You'll probably want to start by searching old headlines in the local papers. Here, I'll show you."

She led me over to a computer connected to the library network and showed me how to search. I wasn't totally sure what I was looking for, but I figured I'd know it when I saw it.

A couple of hours later, I had just one name of a local woman who had been assaulted by a man in our county. The rest of the cases I had read through had sealed the victims' names, understandably, but this woman had intentionally come forward because she "didn't want to be a nameless victim."

I found her on social media and sent her a message, explaining who I was and asking if she would be willing to meet with me. As I pressed send, I wondered if I had lost it completely. Why would a total stranger want to meet with me about the most traumatic experience of her life? Would I have? Probably not. But if it was to put someone like Chris behind bars? Maybe I would.

Hoping that my intuition would prove correct, I logged off the library computer, thanked the librarian who had helped me, and headed back to Mela's. A text from her begging for a coffee and a breakfast bagel had me alter my route back to pick it up on the way.

As I walked anywhere, I always searched for a sighting of Lucas, but there was never one. He was becoming like the Loch Ness Monster, only surfacing when absolutely necessary. Nate knew where his brother lived, but I hadn't gotten that desperate...yet. My time in Florida was going to run out soon, and before then I wanted a proper conversation with him. For now, I had more pressing matters to attend to. Like the starving stomach of my temporary roommate.

I quickened my pace and breathed in the salty sea air as I

weaved in and out of the Saturday morning crowds also enjoying a beautiful sunny day outside. Part of me wondered if my parents had gone to garage sales earlier like they did every Saturday morning, but feelings of nostalgia only clouded my mind, and I couldn't afford to be distracted, so I pushed forward instead.

WHILE I WALKED, I texted back and forth with Ruby. She was supportive of my plan, and it made me miss our late-night chats. We'd texted each other often while I'd been gone, but it wasn't the same as being in our dorm room with snacks and giggles. Fifteen minutes later, I arrived at Mela's with sustenance in hand. She snatched the carefully wrapped bagel from my grip and tore into it with her teeth with feral voracity.

"Sorry, I'm so hungry," she said in her defense at my cry of surprise.

"Uh-huh." I ruffled her dark hair affectionately before moving to sit across from her on the living room couch.

"So, where were you all morning?" Her mouth was full, but I still understood her. She was wearing a pair of her mom's pajamas, and she only wore those when she had a nightmare about her mom's death and couldn't fall back asleep.

"Why didn't you wake me?" I countered, hoping I didn't sound accusatory.

She shrugged. "I've had them so often over the last year that I know what to expect. I have a routine, ya know?" She must have seen something on my face that made her add, "They don't come as often anymore. Only when something stressful is happening, like my best friend being called as a witness in a trial." She smirked playfully, but her eyes still looked haunted.

I moved to sit on the arm of the chair she snuggled in, but she waved me off. "Stop stalling, tell me what you were doing," she demanded.

"Okay, okay."

After filling her in on my morning and the plan that was forming in my mind, I took a sip of my own drink and waited for her verdict.

"It could work," she started, "but do you think she'll meet with you? It's a pretty big ask."

"It is. But I have to try. I can't just sit back and let Chris walk away. Again." I looked out the window and cleared my throat, but Mela saw right through me.

"Aw, Liv, you know that wasn't your fault. None of this was. Chris is a predator, and even if you *had* reported him, his parents would have gotten him off and then Lucas would have a record. Don't blame yourself. I don't. And anyone who does can shove it."

With that, she finished her last bite of bagel and stood up. The fierceness in her eyes lent me a strength I hadn't known I needed. As if through osmosis, she was transferring to me the confidence to let go of my guilt.

I smiled at this strong, brave, beautiful young woman, and considered myself lucky to have a chosen sister like her.

22

We pulled up to a cute bungalow with flowers in every window and a palm tree in the front yard. The grass was lush and green, and a few Nerf guns were strewn about to indicate they had children, though I couldn't be sure how old they were. Nerf guns were a universal toy.

"Is this the place?" Mela asked, though the GPS had clearly told us where to stop.

I nodded, not trusting my voice yet. We got out of the car and walked up the ramp that led to the door. Birds sang gleefully as they flew to and from the feeder that hung outside a large window to the right of the door. Taking a deep breath to steady myself, I knocked three times and then stepped back. A few moments later, the door opened and a man with light brown hair and soft blue eyes who had clearly been on alert ushered us in.

"I'll go get Jacqueline," he called over his shoulder. "She's had a bit of a rough morning." He pointed to a sectional couch, inviting us to sit, and rounded a corner.

My palms were sweaty, and I couldn't seem to shake the tremor in my hands. Mela reached over and gripped my hand tightly, as though reassuring me that I wasn't facing this alone. I squeezed back and she nodded, satisfied that her subliminal message had been received. To distract myself, I let my eyes wander around the room. Stunning full-length canvases of a happy family adorned the room. Jacqueline in a white dress swinging her young daughter by the hands to the girl's delight, then she and her husband gazing into each other's eyes with so much love it made my chest ache. This family looked like one you'd see on an ad for picture frames.

Then Jacqueline appeared in a wheelchair, pushed by the man I now knew to be her husband. The reports I had read said that she was injured in the attack, but surely it couldn't have been to this extent. *There must be another explanation.* I looked from her to the pictures and back again. The woman in the pictures had not been in a wheelchair, so why was she now? My insides twisted at the conclusion my mind was coming up with way too quickly.

"Good morning, ladies. I apologize for not greeting you myself. You've met my husband, Adam?"

She gazed up at him adoringly as he parked her across from us, nodded, and quickly stepped out of the room. He returned just as fast with a glass of water and a bottle of pills. He handed the water to Jacqueline and poured a couple of pills into his hand before giving them to her as well. She swallowed them with difficulty and then sighed with relief as Adam kissed her forehead and turned to us.

"Just a few minutes, please. Her energy is low today." His tone was kind but worried.

"Of course," I mumbled, not knowing what else to say. This had been a mistake. How could I ask Jacqueline to do anything for me?

Mela was making small talk while I snuck glances at the woman before me. She had long straight black hair that shined in the sunlight and a pale complexion. Her eyes were dark and almond shaped, and somehow full of joy as she spoke of her three children—a daughter who was thirteen and two sons aged twelve and ten. The attack had happened eight years before, and now she was in her early forties and paralyzed.

"So, Olivia," she said, "your message sounded urgent."

Our eyes met and I immediately regretted pitying her. The fire in hers told a very different story from the one I was making up in my mind.

I cleared my throat. "Yes, thank you for taking the time to see us on such short notice. And on a Sunday at that. I'm not really sure where to begin," I stammered.

"The beginning is typically the best place." She smiled as she poked fun at me.

I tried to smile back but couldn't quite get there. "I was attacked two years ago, and we're in court right now, but it's not going well." It all came out too quickly, but she seemed to understand.

"The Chris Jamieson case?" Her eyebrows rose with interest.

"Yes. The other witnesses have changed their minds about testifying, so there's only one left…" I trailed off, still unsure of how to make my request. All I could see was the picture behind her, in which she swung her daughter, and her now lifeless legs. "What happened?" The words came tumbling out before I could stop them, and I recoiled in shock at my own boldness.

She nodded sadly. "It's okay, you're allowed to wonder. And given how you found me, I'm sure you've already figured it out."

I shook my head and whispered, "No," even as our eyes locked and I could see the truth in hers. Her attacker had left her paralyzed.

"My husband got a job transfer from North Carolina, and we were new in town. My daughter was five and my sons were four and two. I went out for a walk one night to catch the sunset, and on my way home I was stopped by a man who asked for directions." She paused to take a deep breath and went on, "Before I could even answer, his hands were around my throat, and he slammed my head against a building. When I woke up, I was in the hospital and had been badly beaten…among other things. I couldn't feel my legs anymore, and we all hoped that it was temporary, but it turned out not to be."

She wiped a tear that had slid down her cheek and readjusted herself so that she sat taller.

"In court, his family didn't believe me. They tried to discredit me and ruin my reputation as soon as I came forward. It wasn't the first time he had been accused of attacking women, though my attack was much more severe than the others. I won the case in the end, and now he's behind bars. One less monster on the streets. Looks like this is what it takes, though," she said, looking down at her wheelchair. "Too bad there's no coming back from it."

I cleared my throat again and again as I tried to come up with something to say. "I'm so sorry," was all I could muster.

She asked me about Chris, and I told her what had happened to me and what little I knew of the other victims. It felt ridiculous to even call what happened to me an attack compared to hers, and I fumbled over my words.

"Don't compare our traumas, Olivia," she said as if reading my mind. "What happened to you must have been terrifying. Your lived experience needs no comparison. What happened to each of us was awful in its own way." She smiled at me before asking, "How can I help?"

"Well, I'm not allowed to speak to the other witnesses directly. I wanted to try to convince them to testify because if we don't get Chris put away now, he might…" Abruptly I stopped speaking. Was I really just going to say that?

"He might do what my attacker did to me?" Jacqueline finished my thought, but there was no trace of malice in her tone. More of an understanding that I would have said the truth. "So how can we get through to them?"

"There have been reporters at the courthouse every day of the trial so far. I usually put my head down and walk right past them because our identities are classified, but what if *you* spoke to them? You could tell them your story and urge others to come forward."

"You want me to go to the courthouse?" Her face had paled the moment I suggested it. "I haven't been there since the trial."

Her tone was doubtful.

"Please, Jacqueline," I pleaded. "I'll be with you the whole time. Off to the side, obviously, but there." I wasn't sure how comforted she'd be by that statement, considering I was a nineteen-year-old stranger.

"I will too." Her husband had re-entered the room with impeccable timing. She searched his face, for what I wasn't sure. "If someone had been able to put your attacker behind bars before he did this to you…" His voice was full of anguish as he went on, "How could we not try to help put this *man* behind bars?" He spat the word "man" as though he believed Chris to be anything but, and I agreed with him.

Jacqueline looked from me to her husband, and I held my breath as though everything teetered on the edge of a knife. This was all I had. If she said no, I was out of ideas on how to reach the other witnesses.

"Yes," she said eventually. "But if I'm going to do this, I'm going to do it right." The gleam in her eyes was unmistakable; we were heading to war.

23

"Are you ready for this?" Nate stood beside Mela and across from me outside the courtroom.

"As long as she shows up, I will be," I replied grimly.

Grateful that my parents had opted not to come today, I still found myself looking around to make sure they weren't there. Jacqueline was going to rehash the details of her assault on camera, and I'd be in the background listening to the whole thing; it wasn't something my parents needed to see.

There was still no sign of her, and court was about to start. Johnson had let me know that Chris's defense team was putting some character witnesses on the stand, and I found myself morbidly curious to see what kind of people would come to the defense of a rapist. To be fair, maybe they didn't know he was a monster, but part of me wondered if his parents had paid some people to vouch for him. I certainly wouldn't have put it past them. Maybe that was what they had done to make his old roommate disappear.

The courtroom filled up a lot more slowly than it had on other days, and I was doing my best not to take it as a sign of our impending defeat. Standing at the doors, I shuffled my feet as I played with the bottom of my jacket. It was another one of

Mela's mom's outfits for me today. This one still faintly smelled of her perfume. Sophisticated and sweet, with a hint of citrus. Breathing it in as though I were drawing strength from the scent, I stood a little taller as I continued to scan the hallway for signs of Jacqueline and her husband. My heart noticed the absence of Lucas, but I pushed it aside. There wasn't time to dwell; I had to focus.

Nate and Mela were saving me a seat at the end of a row. I flashed them a grateful look as I did one more sweep of the hallway and went to join them.

"No sign of them?" Mela inquired.

"No," I replied, doing a terrible job of masking my disappointment.

"I'm sure they'll show up. It seemed like they wanted to help, by the sound of it." Nate took a bite of his licorice, and I declined his offer to grab one. I couldn't help but smile at his never-ending optimism.

My smile faded quickly as Chris's defense team began to call their expert witnesses. One after another—psychologists, doctors, mental health experts—testified about the traits of the girls Chris would attract. The type of characteristics his exes all had in common and why that might make us want to lash out at him when things ended. I bit back my vitriol so hard that I could taste blood. Words like unstable, irresponsible, and recluse were thrown around again and again.

For once I was glad that none of the other witnesses were there to hear this insanity. *So we're all unstable recluses, but he's a perfect angel who was just victimized by his exes? Please.* I looked back toward the courtroom doors, and my heart leapt as I saw Jacqueline and her husband at the very back. They looked about as disgusted as I felt after hearing what the "experts" had to say. I caught Jacqueline's eye, and she nodded once as if to say, "He won't get away with this," and I was grateful.

The cross examination of the experts by Johnson and Gunner helped a little, but I feared the damage might be done. I could see a sympathetic look on at least three of the male jurors' faces and one of the females. They were buying that we were unstable girls who weren't sure what had happened but thought we'd cash in on the #metoo movement and destroy the life of a sweet, generous, and kind man. Chris simply had the misfortune of choosing the wrong type of girl. It was outrageous, and I looked to see if even just one of the jury members agreed with me—but the ones who didn't look sympathetic were all stone-faced. I couldn't tell one which way they were leaning.

"...we will reconvene tomorrow morning at nine a.m.," said the bailiff, who had apparently been speaking without my awareness.

My thigh slammed against the side of the bench as I scrambled out of my seat. The reporters were setting up outside of the courtroom doors, and I flew down the aisle, making a beeline for Jacqueline.

"Ready?" I asked through tight lips.

"As I'll ever be."

Her husband wheeled her through the doors, but I stayed hidden just inside of them. I could see and hear what was going on but didn't want to be caught on camera. They headed over to the first journalist, who looked ready to go. A woman I had seen on TV more than once, wearing a bright yellow jacket and slimming black slacks. A look of recognition brightened her face as she saw Jacqueline approaching. Before Jacqueline even said a word, the reporter had already thrust a microphone in her face.

"Miss Hotter? Are you attending this trial because you find any similarities between this case and yours? And how do you feel the implications from the witness testimonies today will affect the verdict?"

Jacqueline answered the questions, strongly condemning the victim-blaming taking place in the court. She expertly navigated her way through the account of similar testimonies that had allowed her own attacker to go free, leading to her assault. Finally, she spoke of the subsequent trial, which had only landed her assailant behind bars because of the random violence that had cost her the use of her legs. The jury had not doubted that a mother of three had never sought to be assaulted by a stranger, although the defense lawyers had previously savaged the young women whom her attacker had raped.

She did it all in under three minutes, captivating the attention of not only the journalist interviewing her, but also the other journalists who had since set up their own cameras to film her as well.

Jacqueline's husband was standing off to the side, and though he looked uncomfortable at the details of his wife's assault, his eyes held a level of admiration and respect I hadn't seen in anyone before.

"Is that what brings you here today?" The original reporter was still asking the questions.

"My assailant's violent streak continued to escalate until he nearly killed me. His defense tried to rip the other victims to shreds, and they had already been traumatized." She gestured to her wheelchair. "It had to come to this before anyone listened. Who knows what he would have done next?"

"Regarding the case against Chris Jamieson, do you believe the same is happening?"

"I wish others had come forward sooner regarding my own case, but what I've realized is that you can only control your own actions. If you don't fight back when someone hurts you, then you'll leave the door open to others getting hurt as well. So I, for one, will be here, supporting every one of his victims until the very end."

It was just the pep talk I needed to keep going. I retreated through the side door I typically took with Johnson, but not before deciding that I would be there until the end too.

24

"Gunner wasn't kidding, that testimony was *weak*." Mela blew her breath out after the last word.

I scolded her under my breath hoping no one else in the courtroom had heard her comment. She shrugged sheepishly and mouthed an apology to me.

Unfortunately, she was right. The last witness, Nicole Herrerra's, testimony hadn't done much but make her seem like a really jealous ex-girlfriend who still wanted Chris back. After what he had done to us, I knew none of us wanted him in our lives, but the defense was doing their best to make it appear otherwise.

The defense lawyers displayed the pomp and arrogance of a football team that had just won the Super Bowl. The last testimony fell in line perfectly with what the "expert" witnesses had testified to a couple of days before. We were unstable ex-girlfriends determined to lump Chris in with the rest of the #metoo attackers and destroy his reputation. Nothing could be further from the truth yet that didn't seem to matter.

Johnson had had to remove the other witnesses from their list, and Chris's defense team knew this last girl was all we had. They destroyed her in the cross examination, and as soon as she was allowed to leave the witness box, she ran crying from the courtroom. The sound of her wails became fainter and fainter the farther away she got. The silence left in her wake felt like a palpable fog intent on choking the life out of me.

Jacqueline had done a few more interviews and even gone on a local podcast, but there was no way to know if her efforts would be enough to convince any of the other witnesses to testify—or even if they'd heard the interviews. The court case was taking over my entire life, and finding balance was a challenge. My body was so weary and heavy that I sank into my seat. My hopes were in the grave, as not a single witness had shown up for court.

"If there's nothing else, we'll reconvene tomorrow morning at ten a.m. for closing remarks." Judge Harper banged her gavel and we all stood as she left.

The bailiff led Chris out of the courtroom, and I couldn't bear to even look at the back of his head, so I looked in the opposite direction, imagining myself somewhere else as I plopped back down on the bench.

"Jacqueline was great on the podcast." Mela interrupted my thoughts. "Maybe some witnesses will come back."

There wasn't much else to do but go back to Mela's and try not to think about what the next day would bring. I decided then and there that if Chris went free, I would get on the next plane back to New York. He wouldn't miss the opportunity to find me and rub his acquittal in my face, and I wanted no part of that. Having made an actual decision, I felt a little better.

"Thanks, Mel," I said as I linked my arm in hers and pulled us both to our feet.

Gunner and Johnson were still at their table, shuffling their papers and murmuring to each other. They kept glancing in my direction, making my pulse quicken and my palms sweat. Johnson nodded me over as the courtroom emptied at a record pace. I wondered how bad what she would say was.

"Olivia, you did a really incredible job on the stand,"

Johnson began. Her tone was one I had heard my mom use many times, right before she gave me bad news. "Unfortunately, it might not be enough to make the charges against him stick."

Her hand was on my shoulder and her gaze searched mine. It was like when the doctor had rested his hand on Mela's shoulder while saying that her mom had died. *Did she understand?* his eyes had seemed to ask. Johnson's eyes were asking mine if I knew what she meant.

I jerked back, involuntarily assaulted by the memory of that day in the hospital. Clearing my throat, I mumbled, "So is there no chance?"

Gunner shook his head solemnly. "Not unless witnesses start dropping out of the sky before tomorrow morning." He stepped around me and then almost as an afterthought leaned over and said, "You did your best, Olivia. We all did."

Later, at Mela's, I poured over the content for my sociology project. I needed a distraction and didn't want to be unprepared when it was time to present it to the class. Logging into my school email account to find a link I had sent to myself, I saw an email from Lucy Marsh. I repeated her name again and again until suddenly I remembered that she was the girl I had talked to outside of Soul Care that day. Not knowing her last name had thrown me off. Tapping on the email, I sat cross-legged on the floor while I read it.

Olivia,

I wanted to thank you for sitting with me that day. It helped more than you know. Your roommate told me why you went back to Florida, and I wanted you to know that it inspired me to contact the district attorney's office that will be prosecuting my ex. I'll be testifying against him during his court case.

See you when you get back.

Lucy

. . .

Tears fell down my face, but they weren't sad ones. All this time, I had felt like my actions had been for nothing. That I hadn't made a difference to anyone. But I had inspired Lucy to testify, and though it didn't help the case against Chris, it mattered. Whatever happened with the case, at least I knew I had done all I could. That would just have to be enough.

I got up before dawn the next morning and made my way to the beach to watch the sunrise. The sky was painted in my favorite bright reds, hot pinks, and flaming oranges. The palm trees stood black, like silhouettes untouched by the light. The ocean waves lapped gently against the sand as I walked along the beach, waiting for the sun to make its grand entrance.

The testimonies were over and there was no need for me to stay. Especially if there was a chance that the charges against Chris would be dismissed. I had already looked up overnight flights. I wasn't running away, but I had put my life on pause to be there. Soon, it would be time to get back to school in New York. That's where my life needed to continue, but for the moment nothing compared to a sunrise over the ocean. I was going to soak it all in while I could.

The red sphere poked its head above the water, and soon a trail of sparkling light extended all the way to my feet in the cool water. I smiled even as my alarm went off and brought me back to the reality of what I was facing. It was time to go back to Mela's and get ready for court.

I breathed in the salty sea air one more time before turning on my heels and heading for the parking lot. I tried to be hopeful, but there wasn't much reason to be. *At least the trial will be over.* That much was true.

25

Mela placed her hand on my bouncing knee while Nate fed me piece after piece of licorice. We were sitting directly behind the district attorney's table and my shoes were making a constant drumming noise as my heels kept tapping against the floor. Johnson threw me a glance that was half annoyance, half pity, and I wasn't sure which I liked less.

I looked back at the courtroom doors for what felt like the hundredth time, but there was still no sign of Gunner. Where could he be? Had he really lost so much faith in this case that he wasn't even going to bother showing up for the last day before deliberations?

We all stood for the judge who had just entered.

"You may be seated." She waved her hand at us.

I watched the judge's mouth turn into a frown when she spotted the empty seat next to Johnson.

"Counselor, where is the other lawyer on your team?" She sounded annoyed. Not a great start to the day.

Johnson cleared her throat before answering. "I believe he's on his way, Your Honor."

"You believe?" The judge's eyebrows were raised, and her

dark eyes seemed to pierce right through Johnson, who shifted uncomfortably from side to side.

"I'm sorry, Your Honor; he told me he was running late and that he would be here as soon as possible."

My face felt hot with secondhand embarrassment for her. Out of the corner of my eye, I saw Mela bite her lip and Nate shove a handful of gummy bears into his mouth. Clearly, they felt it too. The judge gave a frustrated sort of sigh, usually employed by mothers in response to their disobedient children. Just when the silence had stretched the room to its breaking point, Gunner strode through the doors looking slightly disheveled and quickly walked down the aisle to stand next to Johnson.

The judge immediately reprimanded him for his tardiness.

"My apologies, Your Honor. I do have a good reason for my lateness, however." To my surprise, he turned and winked at me discreetly before continuing. "At this time, Your Honor, the prosecution would like to request the presence of more witnesses. Abigail Smythe, Chanel Connors, Amy Mathers, Isabel Silva, and"—he seemed to pause for dramatic effect—"Danny Pintera."

I mustered all my willpower not to stand up and shout. He had found Chris's old roommate, and Danny was willing to testify. They finally had an eyewitness who wasn't one of the victims. Relief swept through me like a flood.

Loud whispers erupted throughout the courtroom as the judge banged her gavel to restore order.

"Objection!" McElroy was red-faced as she argued with the judge. "Your Honor, they can't seriously be trying to add so many witnesses at this late hour."

"Counselors, approach the bench." The judge was shaking her head in evident frustration.

My eyes darted over to Chris. His team of lawyers was soothing him and his parents, as if there was no way this would work. Quickly I leaned forward and whispered to Johnson, who was still in her chair, having let Gunner go up to the judge alone.

"Can they make the judge refuse?" A mix of fear and excitement had started in my stomach and was bubbling its way up into my chest as I waited for her to respond.

She leaned back and whispered her answer. "Oh, no. They'll ask for some time to review statements and prepare their line of questioning. But do you see that guy over there?" She nodded to Chris and went on, "It seems to me he knows it's over for him."

And though I had avoided looking Chris in the eye for the duration of this trial, I finally turned my head to see that his usual composure had been replaced by a crimson face. Our eyes locked and my mouth turned up into a smirk as I gave him a single nod. The kind of nod that said I knew just how screwed he was—and, apparently, so did he. His face grew an even deeper shade of red as he shook his head in disbelief. *Checkmate.*

After several minutes of whispered arguing with the judge, Chris's defense team retreated, and though they were clearly frustrated, they remained professionally courteous. I was hoping for some kind of showdown or outburst from at least one of them. *You're out of order!* Or something equally dramatic.

Chris's mother looked absolutely bewildered that anyone else could have come forward to condemn her precious son. His dad, on the other hand, looked furious that he hadn't done a better job of burying his son's crimes. His scowl had grown so deep that his beady eyes were hardly visible under it. I noticed their legal team was taking great care not to make eye contact with him.

"This trial will take an extended break and resume in two weeks' time, when the new witnesses will take the stand." With that the judge slammed her gavel down and dismissed us.

Leaping out of my seat, I wasn't sure whether to run around to Johnson and Gunner's table or pretend to be unaffected by what had just happened. I turned from one side and back to the other so many times that Mela burst out laughing and slapped my arm.

Gunner and Johnson turned to talk to me, and if it hadn't

been highly inappropriate behavior, I would have thrown myself into Gunner's arms.

"How did you get so many new witnesses to come forward? And Danny?" I demanded.

"I didn't," he replied easily. "You and Jacqueline did." They laughed at the look of shock on my face.

"But I didn't think any of it had an effect," I cried.

"Well, it did. Last night I got calls from witnesses asking if it was too late to come forward. They had either seen the interviews with Jacqueline or listened to the podcast. They were inspired to come forward and half of them—" He collected himself before continuing. "Let's just say their testimonies will make what you and the other witnesses went through look like a walk in the park."

For just a moment he looked haunted by what he had been told the night before. But a moment later, he seemed to collect himself and smiled at me.

"Danny has been overseas, but his sister heard the podcast and knew he had been Chris's roommate, so she called him. Chris had always given her the creeps, and she knew Danny would make a difference in the case. You did good, Olivia. Thanks for refusing to give up."

I simply nodded, as the lump in my throat prevented me from speaking. I eventually managed to ask what would happen next.

Johnson answered: "We'll have a lot of work to do over the next two weeks, but there's no way Chris is getting out of this without some serious jail time. We're going to need you until the end of the trial, though."

I nodded my understanding, and my spirits soared. It had been more than worth it. I only wished that Lucas had been there to see it happen.

All I knew was that I felt a lightness I hadn't known for years, and as I put my arm through Mela's and grabbed Nate for good measure, plans were made in order to celebrate the inevitable demise of a monster.

26

"I'm not sure, Liv. He said something about needing to think. That's all I know, I swear." Nate was holding his hands up as though I was about to attack him.

Another three weeks had gone by, and the trial was officially over. The new testimonies had tipped the balance, and Chris had been sentenced to ten years in jail. I was heading back to New York in the morning. This was my last chance to talk to Lucas alone, and Nate had been gatekeeping his whereabouts for a week. Or maybe he really didn't know where Lucas was, which sounded like the more worrying scenario to me.

"All right, all right. I believe you." I bumped his shoulder with mine on his living room couch to diffuse the tension. Interrogating him for the last twenty minutes had put a chill in the air, and Mela's eyes were shooting daggers at me from across the room.

I checked in the mirror to see that my curls still looked decent, threw on my light jean jacket, and swiped a granola bar for the road. Grabbing Mela's car keys, I headed for the door and called out, "I'm gonna go watch the sunset at the beach," before taking off.

It was a beautiful evening, but I pulled my jacket a little tighter anyway, sort of pulling myself together instead. I thought about heading to the rocks by the lighthouse. That was where *I* liked to think. And then, suddenly, I knew where Lucas would be. It was so obvious I chided myself for not putting it together sooner. I hopped in the car as quickly as I could and the tires squealed as I drove away.

I patted the inside pocket of my jacket and heard the crinkle of the envelope in there. Satisfied that the letter I had written to Lucas was safely tucked away, I drove a little faster. There was no explaining it, but I couldn't shake the feeling that I was running out of time. I pulled into the parking area of Pink Lake just as the sun was low enough not to feel warm anymore. It was where he had brought me the night we made up after I thought he had a girlfriend. And where he had driven to after the whole Chris fiasco.

Only one other car was there, and I didn't recognize it. The driver was leaning against the passenger side away from me. As he heard my car, he turned to look at me and my heart leapt when I saw that it was Lucas. I whipped around his car and parked beside him. Taking a deep breath to steady myself, I gathered my courage and stepped out of the car to face him. His eyes continued to look a little gaunt and his cheeks were slightly sunken. He folded his arms as I stood across from him.

"You're still in town?" His tone was surprised, and that stung. Did he really think I'd have left without saying goodbye? "What? It's not like you haven't left town without saying goodbye before." He laughed, knowing he'd just read my mind, but it wasn't a playful laugh. This one was cynical and unfamiliar.

"You left first last time, actually. You didn't stay after the track meet." I sounded robotic and decided to change the subject before he could answer. I hadn't come here for a fight. "Where's your truck?"

"I tried to give it back to Nate's parents, but they refused to take it. So I sold it and bought this instead. It's more my style, don't you think?" He tilted his head as he waited for my reply.

My eyes raked over his car; it looked at least twenty years old, with duct tape holding one of the mirrors in place. The back passenger door was dented, and the blue paint scratched and faded.

I shrugged. "If you say so, Lucas." This wasn't the boy I knew, but I also believed that he was still in there, somewhere.

"Why did you come, Liv?"

"The trial is over. I wasn't sure if you knew that Chris had gotten ten years." It was the maximum sentence he could have gotten, but it still didn't feel long enough to me.

"He'll probably be out in five for good behavior." Lucas's tone matched my thoughts.

"Yeah. But at least he didn't get off scot-free."

"So, it was all worth it to you, then?" Once more, he didn't mask his surprise.

"If you're asking if I'd do it again, I would. But...I never wanted you to get dragged into it, Lucas. It was so awful watching them rip your life apart on the stand. All you did was try to protect me, and I couldn't do the same. I'm sorry." Tears filled my eyes and I looked away before they fell. I brushed them away quickly, not wanting him to see me crying. I knew that would be worse for him.

I heard him sigh. "It's fine, Liv. It doesn't bother me to hear that I'm trailer trash. I mean, I am."

I wanted to scream at him, but I steadied my voice instead. "Stop saying that. It's the furthest thing from the truth."

"Look, Liv. You might be learning to improve yourself, which is great for you." He almost sounded sincere as he went on, "I've learned to accept myself." His lips turned up into a half smile—and it used to be my favorite one, but I shrank back when I saw his eyes.

"You've learned to accept yourself? It seems more like you've given up on yourself instead. Day drinking? Hardly eating? What happened to football? To living at Nate's? I mean, look at you, Lucas," I cried.

"I was just gonna say, YOU look great. I've never seen your hair curly before. I like it." His voice was filled with irony, and I couldn't even tell if he was being serious or not.

This really couldn't be going any worse.

"I got tired of being their charity case."

His change into vulnerability caught me off guard, and I took a step toward him involuntarily. His eyes widened and I caught myself before moving any closer. Our eyes locked for a moment, but he looked away quickly. I opened my mouth to say something but stopped as I noticed how packed his car was.

"Are you…going somewhere?"

His lips tightened and he looked as though he wasn't going to answer me.

"Where?" I folded my arms to match his.

He shrugged. "Away from here. Like you did. You needed to find yourself and I need to…do the opposite."

"Lose yourself? Lucas, don't talk like that." I wanted to reach out to him, but I made myself resist.

His eyes flashed with anger. "No, you know what? I guess I'm grateful for the trial too. Seeing my life on display like that really showed me how much I haven't amounted to. How no one in my family has done anything with their lives other than end up on government assistance spending any money they have on drugs and alcohol. Or winding up in and out of jail."

"Lucas—"

He talked right over my words.

"Honestly, Liv, I had no right to expect anything more from my life. But just because I'm destined to be a screw up doesn't mean I have to be one here."

"You're not destined to be a screw up. I wish you could see

yourself through my eyes. You don't know how much you helped me when I needed it."

"None of that matters; you get that, right? It may as well have been a lifetime ago."

I swallowed hard. "It matters to me. Doesn't that count for anything?"

"Maybe I'm the prodigal son." He gave another laugh and opened his car door. "Maybe my mom will have a fattened calf waiting for me in the freezer when I get back. Doubt it, though."

I grabbed his hand and hated the way it tensed up. Pulling out the letter from my jacket, I closed his fingers around it and our eyes connected for a moment before he dropped his. I wished that I could break through his barriers, but I knew I couldn't. All I could do was hope that my letter would have some kind of effect on his frozen heart.

He turned away from me and moved to get back into his car.

"Lucas—" My voice caught on the sob that had just snuck to the surface against my will.

His back stiffened and he hesitated as though arguing with himself. I thought I heard him whisper, "Damn it," before he slowly turned back to face me. His eyes were full of emotion, as though I were getting a rare glimpse behind the mask he had so carefully put into place. Quickly he took two steps toward me, and before I knew what was happening, one of his arms was leaning against Mela's car, pushing me into it and the other was wrapped around my waist, pulling me into his chest. His sudden closeness made my breath catch in my throat again. I looked up at him as he touched his forehead to mine. I flung my arms around the back of his neck and closed my eyes as my lips touched his.

Too soon he was pulling away from me. He paused as something caught his eye and gently grabbed the starfish necklace between his fingers. "You still wear it."

"I never took it off."

He released it, and it fell back against my chest as though it weighed a hundred pounds. Wordlessly he got into his car and closed the door behind him. Much as I wanted, this wasn't a journey I could join. Maybe someday our lives would intertwine again, but for now I had to let him go. He glanced at me and smiled in a way that made my insides flop. The conflict on his face made me hope he might change his mind about leaving, but then he shook his head as though to clear it and drove away.

27

I scanned through my cue cards and ensured that my laptop was connected to the giant screen in the front of the room. Checking and rechecking that my slides were all in order, I made sure the music I had chosen for my presentation was queued up properly and wouldn't glitch at the most inopportune time.

"I emailed you that last slide you asked for." Ruby had joined me at the front of the room as students shuffled into the auditorium.

I threw her a grateful smile. "Thank you so much! You're the best."

"Aw, shucks," she responded, and playfully bumped my arm with her elbow.

Am I ready for this? It was the twentieth time I had asked myself that question. Though I knew that the answer was yes, absolutely, I was still nervous. Excited, for sure, but nervous.

"You're gonna be great, Liv. Don't sweat it." Ruby was studying me as I wrung my hands together.

"I just want to do them justice, ya know? I can't help but feel like they'll be watching." Knowing how stupid it sounded, I grimaced to myself.

"Your ancestors? Oh, no doubt. I'd be watching if it were me."

"Gee, thanks," I replied while rolling my eyes.

She placed her hand on my shoulder and turned me toward her. "Seriously, Liv. They'd be proud of you. I know I am." She smiled and went to take a seat, leaving me alone with my thoughts.

I clicked through the slides of my presentation to see again that all the text prompts were right. It made me smile to think about how far I had come since the beginning of the school year. I thought back to how afraid I had been before the trial started, and how lost I had still felt. That wasn't me anymore.

This presentation was about so much more than my ancestors' journey out of slavery. It also represented my own journey to find my place in the world. To realize that I no longer needed validation from my biological parents to feel like I belonged here. In fact, I never had.

Someone waved at me from near the middle of the auditorium, and a smile stretched across my face as I saw that it was Lucy and some of the other girls from Soul Care. Even Professor Powell was squeezing between students to sit with them. I couldn't mask the surprise on my face, and she caught it and winked in response.

Lucy's eyes connected with mine, and I remembered how moved I was by her email. If only more women had experiences like that: someone helping them feel seen and, in turn, inspiring them to take action. As I continued to flip through my cue cards, it dawned on me that that was exactly what had happened for me too. Learning about Mary's courage had helped me find my own. I looked at a picture of Harriet Tubman standing in front of the church my ancestors had helped build. *No one is born courageous,* I realized. It's not like anyone sprang out that way at birth. They had to choose it when the opportunity arose. The same way I found the courage to stand up to Ali, fight for my relationship with G.G., and refuse to give up on my friendship with Leah in the process.

So often people talked about courageous people as though they had always been that way, but I knew now that wasn't true. People became brave…or—and I thought of Chris as the words came to mind—they became cowards. Just like how a silversmith melts the silver to remove the dross, or a diamond is formed under intense pressure, courageous people are tested and strengthened by all they go through. Maybe that was the reason we went through terrible things. Maybe this was all some beautiful ripple effect orchestrated by something unseen. The hairs on my arms stood straight. No one knew the way; I could see that. We were all just trying to figure it out as we went along. But I now realized that if you didn't give up, you'd eventually find it.

Gathering my cue cards, I stood a little taller. I was proud to tell my class this story. And, more surprisingly, I was proud of myself too. It had been a hell of a year, and though the many ups and downs had made it feel like I was strapped to a ride I didn't want to be on, I figured I'd look back on this year with fondness. A year that helps to define you doesn't come along often, after all.

I thought I had come to New York to become the kind of person who deserved to have friends like Mela, Nate, and Lucas. What I realized was that I had always been that person. This year had showed me who I already was, and what I was made of. It had showed me where I came from and the kind of courage and strength I was fortunate enough to have inherited.

I waved to my professor, signaling that I was ready to begin my presentation. The auditorium was packed, and my nerves had begun to make me jittery.

Water? Check.

Slide show loaded? Check.

Music queued up? Check.

Laptop connected to the projector? Check.

Looks like I'm as ready as I'll ever be. I loaded up my slide show onto the projector and nodded at Ruby. She dimmed the lights for me, and I took a deep, steadying breath.

"Hi, everyone! Thanks for being here. I want to share with you a little story. This is the story of how Harriet Tubman made it possible for me to be here today…"

EPILOGUE

Olivia Rose Jackson - July 1st

"Here you go," I said as I handed the clipboard back to the receptionist.

"Okay, great. Can I see your identification so I can issue you a pass?"

"Yes, of course." I handed her my driver's license and waited impatiently for her to finish checking me in.

The art on the walls hadn't changed much since the last time I'd been there. The sun was pouring into the large lobby, but I paid little attention to my surroundings. All I wanted was to get my pass and be let in already.

"Here you go, Miss Jackson. You just need to head straight through those do—"

I pulled the badge out of her hands as gently as I could without snatching it away the way I wanted to. "Oh yes, thank you. I know the way."

She looked taken aback, so I smiled sweetly at her and forced myself to walk at a normal pace toward the electronic double doors. I tapped my badge on the scanner and a loud buzzer sounded as the locks clicked open. Pushing my way through the door, I practically raced down the hallway, surprising more than one guest. A cry of, "Oh my heavens!" as a lady in a wheelchair clutched her chest made me slow down to a walk, lest I gave anyone a heart attack.

Walking by the common room, I glanced out the large bay window overlooking the courtyard. It had been ages since I'd seen this room, and I'd forgotten how vast it was with its cathedral ceiling, exposed wooden beams, and elaborate chandeliers hanging at every few feet.

I rounded the corner and came up to the French doors that led out to the garden. Once I got through the doors, I could see her sitting off in the distance at one of the small tables. My face broke into a wide grin as I strode towards her. She looked a little frailer than the last time I had seen her, but a plate of shrimp and a bowl of sauce sat on the table, and I laughed out loud at the sight. *Some things never change.*

She heard the sound and looked up in surprise. As soon as she saw me, her face broke into such a wide grin, it must have matched my own.

I ran over and threw my arms around her. "I missed you, G.G." My voice was thick with emotion.

"I missed you too, my sweet Olivia. I could hardly believe it when Ali told me she'd reinstated your privileges."

"I wasn't sure she would, but she gave me her word. It's nice that she kept it."

"Yes, yes, there may be hope for her yet." G.G.'s eyes crinkled and she held my hand tightly and demanded to know everything that had happened since we'd last spoken.

It had been a hard-fought battle, but seeing her smile and hearing her laugh again made it all worth it to me. I knew without a doubt that Mary would have been proud.

LUCAS:

EIGHTEEN MONTHS. It seemed like a lifetime ago but also just like yesterday.

Had it really been so long since I'd been back in Florida? I was directed to join a line beside a conveyor belt, where other people were taking off their shoes and placing their belongings into a plastic bin to be x-rayed. Following suit, I kicked off my shoes and dropped them into the bin nearest me. A few people were in front of me, so I pulled out the letter to read it one last time.

Dear Lucas,
I love you. I should have told you that day on the beach when you said it to me. I've regretted that moment ever since. It never mattered to me where or how you grew up. You'll never be trash to me. Exactly the opposite, actually. You are the boy who helped me find myself when I was lost beyond recognition. I hope that someday I can help you do the same.

Love, Liv

I SHOULD HAVE STAYED, I told myself for the hundredth time. A uniformed agent with latex gloves was ushering me forward toward the metal detector.

"You've got to put ALL of your belongings in before you go through," he snapped at me, eyeing the letter in my hand suspiciously like I was going to turn it into a ninja star and use it to make my escape out of the line.

I folded it back into its familiar creases and carefully put it into the bin he was impatiently pointing to. Shuffling through the metal detector, I breathed a sigh of relief when no alarms sounded. Any time I went through one, I worried it'd go off like I had forgotten to take a fifty-inch TV out of my pants first.

Another uniformed agent beckoned to me and had me open my arms and spread my legs so he could wave his hand-held metal detector over every inch of me. It seemed a little overkill, but I was in no position to complain.

After putting my shoes back on, I glanced up and saw some signs overhead directing me while another uniform tailed my every move. Where he thought I might go was beyond me. We walked for a long time through a narrow, windowless hallway with florescent lighting, our footsteps the only sound echoing off the bare walls. A few minutes later, we stepped into a much larger room with some tables set up. A few guys were playing cards at one, and at another they held an arm-wrestling match. I didn't let my gaze wander too much for fear of catching someone's eye accidentally.

"This is you." The uniform had stopped and nodded me on.

I walked into a small room and looked around, feeling claustrophobic. There was a bunk bed, toilet, and sink, all fastened to the cement walls. The lightbulb above the sink had a cage around it, and there were more tick marks on the walls than I could count. For two years less a day, this was going to be my new home.

A loud buzzer sounded and a mechanical door with shiny iron bars slid closed behind me, sealing my fate. I turned around to grip the bars and they were cold in my palm. The uniform's footsteps grew fainter as he moved down the hall.

Turning around, I caught my reflection in the dirty mirror and winced at the way the orange jumpsuit made my face look even paler than usual. I walked over to the wall, picked the piece of chalk that had been left behind off the ground, and added my first tally mark.

Well, the good news is, this is definitely rock bottom.

PRE-ORDER BOOK 4 NOW!

Order Your signed copy of Redeemed today!

Order the e-book on Amazon here:

ACKNOWLEDGMENTS

First and foremost I'd like to thank my biological father, James, for being willing to have tough conversations with me and love me through them. Jesus you're my rock and that will never change. To my family, thank you for not being offended when I put my noise cancelling headphones on and ignore the world in order to write. You are my delights. To my best friend and business partner Lauren, thank you for loving me at my best and at my most unhinged, and never judging me for any of it. Cee, what can I say? You are my favorite editor and your constant pushing me to be better is both frustrating and the best thing to ever happen to me. Never change. Esther, you brought this series to life with your cover designs. I am forever grateful. To my beta readers and ARC team, thank you for reading early copies! And to every single reader who picked up this series and gave this indie author a chance, thank you from the bottom of my heart. You have made the biggest difference in my life. If you'd be willing to leave a review on Amazon and/or Goodreads it would mean the world to me.

ABOUT THE AUTHOR

Meggan Larson is an award winning author (best selling on Amazon), course creator, wife, mom, and adoptee. She currently lives in Ottawa, Canada with her husband and three children. Through her indie publishing company, Starfish Stories Publishing, she helps the girl who reads all the books become the woman who writes and publishes them.

She lives her life around the concept of the starfish story, where a woman is tossing washed up starfish back into the ocean as they lay dying on the shore, and someone comes along and scoffs at her. He tells her she can't possibly make a difference because there are thousands and she'll never get to them all in time. She picks one up, tosses it back into the water, and says,

"It made a difference to that one."

Meggan wants to make a difference, even if it's just for one person.

Connect with her at hello@megganlarson.com or at her website at https://megganlarson.ca

Jump on her mailing list:

ALSO BY MEGGAN LARSON

Adopted - Book #1 in the Adopted series

Fractured - Book #2 in the Adopted series

Redeemed - Book #4 in the Adopted series

The Truth About Forgiveness (non fiction)

The Truth About Finding Joy in the Darkness (Anthology)

The Truth About Success (Anthology)

Being & Belonging (Anthology)

Starfish Stories, An Anthology Volume One

Excuse You? (A memoir)

Portraits (Anthology)

ABOUT STARFISH STORIES PUBLISHING

Starfish Stories Publishing: "Where the woman who reads all the books becomes the woman who writes them."

The Starfish Stories Publishing Company was founded in 2022. Its mission is to create a ripple effect of impact in the world through beautiful storytelling, authentic vulnerability, and inspiring messages of hope and belonging in a world desperate for real connection.

If you have a manuscript you would like us to consider, tap the QR code below and let's chat!